'This is why you isn't it?' he demanded. 'You are determined to destroy me.'

'No,' she protested, as the robe fell to the floor, but Demetri wasn't listening to her. His fingers slid over her shoulders and down her back, caressing her hipbones briefly, before moving onto her bottom. Filling his hands with the rounded globes, he brought her deliberately against him.

'Do you have any idea what it's like to be this close to you and not be a part of you?' he asked, his voice thick with emotion. 'You drive me crazy,' he went on. 'Stark, staring crazy, and I still want you even closer to me, under me, to give me some relief from this torment you're putting me through.'

'Demetri, please—'

The husky tone of her voice vibrated through him, but he was too far gone to listen to reason. Tucking a hand beneath the tumbled silk of her hair, he tipped her head up to his, his mouth silencing any further protest.

New York Times bestselling author **Anne Mather** has written since she was seven, but it was only when her first child was born that she fulfilled her dream of becoming a writer. Her first book, CAROLINE, appeared in 1966. It met with immediate success, and since then Anne has written more than 150 novels, reaching a readership which spans the world.

Born and raised in the north of England, Anne still makes her home there, with her husband, two children and now grandchildren. Asked if she finds writing a lonely occupation, she replies that her characters always keep her company. In fact, she is so busy sorting out their lives that she often doesn't have time for her own! An avid reader herself, she devours everything from sagas and romances to mainstream fiction and suspense. Anne has also written a number of mainstream novels, with DANGEROUS TEMPTATION, her most recent title, published by MIRA® Books. If you would like to write to Anne, please e-mail her at mystic-am@msn.com

Recent titles by the same author:

THE PREGNANCY AFFAIR

THE GREEK TYCOON'S PREGNANT WIFE

BY
ANNE MATHER

MILLS & BOON®
Pure reading pleasure

First published in Great Britain 2007
Harlequin Mills & Boon Limited,
Eton House, 18-24 Paradise Road, Richmond, Surrey TW9 1SR

© Anne Mather 2007

ISBN 978 0 263 85349 0

Set in Times Roman 10¼ on 12¾ pt
01-0907-50363

Printed and bound in Spain
by Litografia Rosés, S.A., Barcelona

THE GREEK
TYCOON'S
PREGNANT WIFE

CHAPTER ONE

JANE let herself into her apartment and headed straight for the fridge. It might be empty of anything to eat, but she knew she'd left a half-pack of colas on the shelf. Pulling out one of the chilled cans, she flipped the tab and drank. Then, savouring its coolness on her tongue, she kicked off her shoes and walked back into the living area.

It was good to be home, she thought, looking round the large space that served as both living and dining room. She was glad now she'd had the builder knock down the wall that had once separated the two rooms. Together with a small service kitchen, her bedroom and the adjoining bathroom, it had been her home for the past five years.

She'd dropped her suitcase in the small entry hall and as she went to retrieve it, she saw the message light blinking on her answering machine. Her mother, she thought resignedly. Mrs Lang would be anxious to hear that her daughter had arrived home safely. Even though she was familiar with the internet and would no doubt have checked flight arrivals at Heathrow, she still needed the confirmation of Jane's voice to assure her that all was well.

Sighing, Jane pressed the key to retrieve her messages and waited patiently for Mrs Lang's recorded voice to speak. Her friends knew she was away, and all business calls would be routed to the gallery. So she was unprepared when a disturbingly familiar male voice spoke her name.

'Jane? Jane, are you there? If you are, pick up, will you? *Ineh poli simandiko.*' It's important.

Jane sank down weakly onto the small ottoman she kept beside the phone. Despite her determination never to let Demetri Souvakis into her life again, she couldn't deny that his rich dark voice with its distinctive accent still had the power to turn her weak at the knees.

But then, it wasn't his voice that had made him a millionaire several times over before his twenty-fifth birthday. That had come from his heritage and his complete ruthlessness in business, she reminded herself, a ruthlessness that had somehow spilled over into his private life.

Jane expelled an unsteady breath now and was still trying to calm her racing pulse when a second message started. 'It's me, Jane,' he said. 'Your husband. *Theos*, I know you're there. Don't make me have to come looking for you. Can't we at least deal with one another like civilised adults?'

That helped. The arrogance in his voice, the way he just assumed she'd be available whenever he chose to contact her. And how could he call himself her husband when for the past five years he hadn't cared if she was dead or alive?

Her nails dug into her palms in her efforts to control the anger that swept through her, but that didn't stop the painful memories from tearing her hard-won objectivity to shreds. How dared he contact her now as if he had some right to do so? As far as she was concerned, she'd cut him out of her life.

Well, almost.

She sighed. She remembered when she'd first encountered his father at the gallery where she'd worked in London. Leo

Souvakis had been so charming, so polite. He'd explained that he was looking for a piece of sculpture to take back to Greece, a bronze, if possible, to match the other pieces he'd collected over the years.

Jane had only been working at the gallery for a short time, but already she'd begun to show an aptitude for recognising talent when she saw it. And the delicate sculpture of the goddess Diana by a virtually unknown artist seemed an appropriate choice to make.

Leo Souvakis had been delighted, both by the piece and by Jane, and they'd been discussing the relative merits of oriental pottery and porcelain when Demetri Souvakis had appeared...

Jane shook her head. She so much didn't want to think about this now. She'd just come back from a very successful trip to Australia and Thailand and what she really wanted to do was go to bed. She'd been travelling for the better part of fourteen hours, the unexpected layover in Dubai not part of her agenda.

She was just about to get up, determined not to be intimidated, when a third message began. 'Jane? Are you there, darling? I thought you told me you'd be home by eight o'clock. It's half-past now and I'm getting worried. Ring me as soon as you get in. I'll be waiting.'

Putting all thought of her other calls to the back of her mind, Jane reached for the receiver. Pressing the pre-set key, she waited only a couple of rings before her mother picked up. 'Hi, Mum,' she said, trying to inject a note of confidence into her voice. 'Sorry you've been worried. The plane made an unscheduled stop in Dubai.'

'Oh, I see.' Mrs Lang sounded relieved. 'I thought it might be something like that. So, are you OK? Did you have a good trip? You'll have to tell me all about it over lunch.'

Lunch? Jane only just managed to suppress a groan. There

was no way she was going to feel up to having lunch with her mother today. 'Not today,' she said apologetically, knowing Mrs Lang wouldn't take kindly to her refusal. 'I'm beat, Mum. I need at least eight hours of sleep before I do anything else.'

Her mother tutted. 'Eight hours. Really, Jane, I rarely get more than four hours a night! Didn't you sleep on the plane?'

'Not much.' Jane wished she were less honest. 'How about lunch tomorrow, Mum? That'll give me time to come round.'

There was silence for a moment, and then Mrs Lang said, 'You've been away for almost three weeks, Jane. I'd have thought you'd want to see your mother. Particularly as you know I'm stuck in this house most of the day.'

Whose fault is that? Jane was tempted to ask, but she didn't want to start an argument. 'Why don't you ask Lucy to have lunch with you?' she suggested instead. 'I'm sure she'd jump at the chance.'

'I'm sure she would, too.' But Mrs Lang was not enthusiastic. 'Besides, if your sister comes here for lunch, I'll have Paul and Jessica running all over the house.'

'They are your grandchildren, Mum.'

'Yes, and they're totally undisciplined.'

'Oh, Mum…'

'Anyway, if you can't be bothered to visit your mother, I'll have to make do with my own company.' Mrs Lang sniffed. 'What a shame! I wanted to tell you who came to see me last week.'

Demetri!

Jane expelled a calming breath. 'You had a visitor?' she asked, trying to sound only vaguely interested. 'Well, that was nice.'

'It wasn't *nice* at all,' her mother snapped angrily. Then, with a sound of impatience, 'Oh, I suppose he told you. Is he the reason I'm being put off until tomorrow?'

'No!' Jane caught her breath. 'But I assume you're talking

about Demetri. He left a couple of messages on my machine. When he couldn't get an answer, he must have guessed you'd know where I was.'

'Which, of course, I did.'

'Did you tell him?' Jane was wary.

'I said you were abroad,' declared Mrs Lang tersely. 'I hope you didn't expect me to lie for you, Jane.'

'No.' Jane sighed. 'Did he say what he wanted to speak to me about?'

'As I said earlier, if you want to hear all about it, you'll have to wait until you have time for me in your busy schedule. You know I don't like discussing family matters over the phone.' She paused. 'I'll expect you tomorrow, shall I?'

Jane gritted her teeth. She so didn't need this. She'd had a successful trip and she'd been looking forward to taking a couple of days break before having to return to the gallery. Now she felt compelled to go and see her mother, if only to find out what this was all about.

'How about supper?' she asked, knowing Mrs Lang was going to love this. Having her eldest daughter over a barrel was one of the joys of her life. It so rarely happened these days, although when Jane had been living with Demetri she'd constantly been aware that her mother was waiting for the marriage to fail. When it had, she'd been there to pick up the pieces, though Jane had known there'd been a measure of satisfaction in being proved right once again.

'Supper?' she echoed now. She considered. 'Tonight, you mean?'

It was a game, Jane knew, but she was too tired to play it. 'Whenever suits you,' she said wearily. 'Leave a message when you've made up your mind.'

'Now, is that any way to treat your mother?' But Mrs Lang

seemed to realise it was time to back off. 'Tonight will be fine, darling,' she said serenely. 'Shall we say seven o'clock? Or is that too early for you?'

'Seven's OK.' Jane's tone was flat. 'Thanks, Mum. I'll see you then.'

It was a relief to hang up the receiver and, when the phone rang again before she could move away, she snatched it up with a definite edge to her voice. But it was only a cold call, asking her if she was interested in buying a new kitchen, and she slammed it down with a definite feeling of exploitation.

Of course, she realised belatedly, it could have been Demetri, but she didn't think that was likely. Demetri was no doubt in London on business and he'd have no time to think about his estranged wife if he had meetings to attend. She would come fairly low on his agenda. As she'd always done, she thought bitterly. Judging by his tone of voice, she had no reason to think he'd changed.

Sighing, she abandoned any idea of unpacking until later and trailed into the bathroom to take a quick shower. She looked exhausted, she thought, tucking strands of honey-blonde hair back behind her ears. Gazing into the mirror, she wondered how much she'd changed in the last five years. There were tiny lines fanning out from the corners of her eyes, but her skin was still smooth in other places. Of course, she'd gained a couple of inches around her hips, which was annoying, but her breasts were firm even if they'd filled out, too.

Oh, well, who cares? she thought, too tired to even dry herself properly after her shower. Twisting her still damp hair into a loose knot on top of her head, she tumbled naked between the sheets. And not even her worries about why Demetri might want to see her could keep her eyes open.

The phone awakened her. At least, she thought it was the

phone, but when she groped for the extension beside the bed the ringing still went on. It was the doorbell, she realised. Someone wanted access to one of the apartments and was probably ringing every bell in the building until they got lucky.

Sighing, she flopped back against the pillows and looked at the clock on the bedside cabinet. It was almost noon. She'd slept for less than four hours, but that was something, she supposed. Amazingly, she didn't feel as tired as she'd done when she flew east. Coping with jet lag was always easier in this direction.

The bell rang again and, throwing back the covers, Jane slipped her arms into the sleeves of a green silk wrapper. Then, padding across the living room to the intercom, she lifted the handset. 'Yes?'

'Jane?' It was Demetri, and her stomach made a sickening dive. 'Jane, I know it's you. *Hristo*, will you open the door?'

Jane didn't move. She couldn't. She felt frozen. The faint sense of disorientation she'd felt when she'd first woken up seemed to be paralysing her ability to speak. It was too soon, she thought. She needed time to pull herself together. If she'd ever considered encountering her estranged husband again, she'd assumed it would be on her terms, not his.

'Jane!' She heard him swear in his own language. 'Jane, I know you're in there. Your mother was kind enough to tell me you'd be home today.' His voice was becoming more impatient. 'Come on, open the door. Do you want me to be arrested for soliciting or some such thing?'

Anyone less likely to allow himself to be arrested for soliciting Jane could hardly imagine. Demetri Souvakis was far too sure of himself for that. Besides which, that was just an excuse to get her to press the release button. Her fellow flatmates were evidently out at work—or shopping in the case of Mrs Dalladay—and she was his only means of access.

'I'm not even dressed yet, Demetri,' she blurted at last, aware that her voice had a breathy sound to it. It was all she could think of to say, but it wasn't enough.

'*Aghapita*, seeing you naked is nothing new to me,' he reminded her drily. 'Come. I've been trying to reach you for the better part of a week. We can't all spend half the day in bed.'

That got her juices flowing again. 'I've just flown over six thousand miles, Demetri,' she told him tartly. 'And if I remember correctly, you don't do jet lag very well yourself.'

'Ah, yes. *Signomi*. Sorry.' But he didn't sound it. 'I guess that was thoughtless. Put it down to frustration. I'm not very good at that either.'

'Tell me about it.' Jane tried to sound sardonic. 'How are you, Demetri? Still as impatient as ever, I see.'

'*Theos*, I have been patient, *ghineka*. Now, are you going to open up, or must I break down this—' there was a pause while he obviously endeavoured to control his anger '—this door?'

Jane's jaw took on a stubborn curve. She badly wanted to call his bluff. Only the embarrassment she would suffer if he made good on his threat deterred her, and without another word she jabbed a finger onto the button.

There was a low buzz as the door downstairs was released and then the sound of footsteps on the stairs. Heavy footsteps, climbing the stairs with a speed that had her retreating to the far side of the living room. She'd left the door ajar and, although she told herself she didn't care what he thought of her, it occurred to her belatedly that she hadn't even brushed her hair since she'd tumbled so unexpectedly out of bed.

She was finger-combing it behind her ears when Demetri appeared in the doorway. Tall and lean, with the thick dark hair of his ancestors, he too looked older, she reassured herself. But despite the threads of grey at his temples, his face, with its familiar trace of dark stubble, was tougher, harder than she remembered, but just as attractive.

His presence had lost none of its impact, reminding her of the day he strode into the gallery, looking for his father. When the old man had introduced them he'd been polite, but hardly flattering, treating her with a cool indifference she'd half resented then.

Now Demetri paused in the doorway, and then stepped into the apartment. So this was where she lived, he thought broodingly. He'd heard she was doing well at her job. He couldn't help admiring the huge expanse of living space that swept from the front to the back of the old Victorian building. The sun pouring in from the windows at each end filling the place with a watery light.

But for all his irritation at the way she'd kept him waiting outside, it was to Jane that his eyes were irresistibly drawn. She stood the width of the room away, her arms wrapped protectively about herself. She was wearing a silk robe that she was holding tightly around her. As if he'd threatened her, he reflected, disliking the notion. For pity's sake, what was she expecting him to do? Jump her bones?

'Jane,' he said, before that idea could take hold and destroy his detachment, and her lips, which she'd been pressing together, relaxed a little. She looked good, he thought unwillingly. Too good to a man who was planning to marry another woman as soon as he was free. But then, Jane had always had that effect on him. It was why he'd married her, for God's sake. Why he'd been so reluctant to find another woman to take her place.

Why his mother had been so opposed to him doing this himself!

'Demetri,' Jane responded stiffly, and when he leaned against the door to close it she stood a little taller, as if bracing herself for whatever was to come.

She wasn't wearing any make-up, of course, and he suspected the colour in her cheeks owed more to a mental rather than a physical source. Green eyes, which used to haunt his sleep, as clear as the mountain-fed lakes on Kalithi.

'How have you been?' he asked, straightening away from the door, and Jane's mouth went a little dry when he moved further into the room. He had an indolent grace of movement that made anything he wore look like a designer item, though she guessed the casual cargo pants and black leather jacket were the real thing.

He was still wearing his wedding ring, she noticed. The wedding ring she'd bought him when they'd exchanged their vows in the small chapel on Kalithi, the island his family owned and where he lived when he wasn't flying around the world attending to the demands of his shipping empire. His father had retired before they'd married, much against his mother's wishes. But then, she'd never wanted Demetri to marry an English girl, particularly one who had opinions of her own.

'I'm OK,' she said now, forcing a tight smile. 'Tired, of course. But then, I haven't had much sleep in the last twenty-four hours.'

'And I woke you up?' Demetri came to stand beside one of a pair of mulberry printed sofas that faced each other across a taupe rug. It was the only floor covering at this end of the room, the stripped maple floor requiring little adornment. A dark brow arched in reluctant apology. 'I'm sorry about that.'

'Are you?' Jane gave an indifferent shrug. 'So, do you want to tell me what you're doing here, Demetri? You didn't come here just to pass the time of day. You said it was important.'

Demetri averted his eyes, concentrating instead on his fingers massaging one of the sofa cushions. 'It is,' he said flatly.

Then he lifted his head again, giving her a look out of night-dark eyes, causing a shiver of apprehension to slide down her spine. 'I want a divorce, Jane. Is that straight enough for you?'

CHAPTER TWO

NOW it was Jane's turn to look away from his cold stare. Despite her best efforts, she was trembling, and she hoped like hell that he couldn't see it.

It wasn't a total shock to her, of course. For years after their separation she'd lived with the very real expectation that sooner or later Demetri was going to want his freedom. She was sure his mother would persuade him, if no one else. And she'd wanted it, too, in those days. But somehow, with the passage of time, she'd actually begun to believe that it was never going to happen.

'You OK?'

Dammit, he had noticed. And he was coming across the room towards her. Jane had to get out of there, and fast, before he started feeling sorry for her. She didn't think she could bear that.

'Let me get dressed,' she said, speaking without breathing, knowing that if she sucked in a gulp of air the sobs that were rising in her throat would choke her.

'Janie…'

The name he used to call her when he was making love to her was almost her undoing. 'Just give me a minute,' she said and, opening the door into her bedroom, she closed it firmly behind her.

But once she was alone, she couldn't prevent the storm of

emotion that engulfed her. Hot tears streamed down her cheeks and, with her nose running too, she groped her way across the room to the bathroom. Grabbing a handful of tissues from the box she kept there, she endeavoured to staunch the salty flow, sinking down onto the toilet seat and burying her face in her hands.

'*Agapita*—'

She didn't know how long she'd been sitting there when he spoke. Dear God! Her head jerked up in disbelief. Demetri was standing in the bathroom doorway watching her and she knew she'd never felt so humiliated in her life.

'Get out!' she choked, struggling to get to her feet. 'How—how dare you come in here? You have no right to invade my privacy like this.'

Demetri merely sighed and propped his shoulder against the frame of the door. Then he regarded her with disturbing gentleness. 'I dare because I care about you,' he said, his accent thickening with emotion. '*Theos*, Janie, how was I to know you'd react like this? I'd have thought you'd be glad to get me out of your life.'

Jane sniffed. 'I am.'

'It looks like it.'

'Oh, don't flatter yourself, Demetri. I've just flown halfway around the world and I'm exhausted.' It was an effort but she managed a tight smile. 'It was a shock. I don't deny it. But I'm not crying because I'm—heartbroken. Far from it.'

Demetri didn't look convinced. 'So—what? You usually break down like this when you get back from a trip? Is that what you're saying?'

'Don't be even more of a jerk than you have to be,' Jane retorted, struggling to regain a little of her composure. 'OK. What do you want me to say, Demetri? That I'm—crushed? Desolated? That hearing the arrogant louse I married is going to inflict himself on some other poor female has devastated me?' She managed a harsh laugh. 'Don't hold your breath.'

Despite himself, Demetri was angered by her words. He'd come to find her with the best of intentions, he told himself, and now here she was, tearing his good will to shreds. That was so like Jane: shooting first and regretting it later. Only something told him that this time she wasn't about to back down.

He straightened. 'You're an ungrateful bitch, do you know that?' he snapped, his hands clenching into fists at his sides.

'So you've told me,' she retorted, scrubbing her cheeks with the tissues one last time before flushing them down the lavatory.

'Well, perhaps you ought to curb your tongue,' he muttered. 'My lawyer tells me that in the circumstances, I don't have to offer you anything by way of a settlement.'

Jane's lips parted. 'I don't want your money. I never did!' she exclaimed scornfully. 'Just get out of here. I want to get dressed.'

Demetri stared at her. For all her air of bravado, he was fairly sure she wasn't half as confident as she was trying to appear. Those incredible green eyes still shimmered with unshed tears, and her mouth—the mouth he'd kissed so many times—couldn't quite hide its tremor.

And, although her words had irritated him beyond all reason, he found himself saying, 'If that's what you want?'

'What else is there?'

Tilting her head up to his, Jane stared back at him and he felt an unwilling twinge of admiration for the way she was handling herself now. A twinge of admiration, yes—and something else, something he didn't even want to put a name to. Something that had him suddenly moving to close the space between them.

The bath was at her back and Jane had nowhere to go. So when he put out his hand and looped his fingers behind her neck, she could only stand there and let him look down at her with what she was sure was a mixture of amusement and derision in his eyes.

'How about this?' he suggested, his voice rougher than before, and, before she could anticipate what he was about to do, he'd bent towards her and covered her mouth with his.

Jane didn't know how she stopped her legs from buckling beneath her. It was so long since Demetri had touched her, so long since she'd felt those long fingers against her skin. Heat was coming off him in waves, enveloping her in its sensual embrace, and, although she'd determined not to close her eyes, seeing the closeness of his long lashes, the dusky shadow of his jawline, she so much wanted to do so and sink into his kiss.

But how could that be? A moment ago they'd been dumping on one another, and now—now she was letting him touch her, kiss her, push his thigh between her legs as if she wasn't throbbing there already.

It had to be because she'd been crying, she told herself, trying to rationalise something that refused to be rationalised. She was always twice as emotional when she'd been crying and Demetri knew that very well. Oh, yes, who better? He'd made her cry so many times before…

But right now that didn't seem half as important as it should, and when he said, 'Ah, *mora*,' right against her mouth, her lips parted on a breath of submission. And then his tongue was in her mouth, sweeping intimately over hers, taking possession with a hunger that was far too appealing.

Demetri trailed his lips across her cheek, savouring the lingering taste of her tears. Her skin was soft, smooth, endlessly fascinating, and he slid an arm around her waist and pulled her close against him.

Sanity seemed to have deserted him. The reasons why he'd

come here blurred by the depth of his sudden desire. His hand found the cord of her robe, loosened it, allowed the sides to fall apart. Then he was gazing at full round breasts, their peaks as hard in the flesh as they'd looked outlined beneath the silk.

With heavy-lidded eyes he watched himself cup one swollen globe in his hand, let his thumb rub over the sensitive nipple with an urgency that bordered on violence, and he swore. '*Skata*, Jane,' he groaned, suspecting even then that he was going to regret this. But, *Theos,* she was where he wanted her to be, nestled against him, causing him a hard-on that was in danger of giving him a heart attack if he didn't relieve the pressure soon.

Jane swayed, her own emotions rushing dangerously close to meltdown. She couldn't let him do this, she told herself. She had to get away from him. But when she moaned into his mouth, Demetri sensed she wanted him to go on.

Her robe was off her shoulders now, and, when he swept her up into his arms and carried her into the adjoining bedroom, she felt it slip away onto the floor. Then she was on her back on the bed that was still warm from when she'd left it. Demetri was tearing off his jacket and T-shirt, exposing the muscled strength of his hard brown flesh to her distracted gaze.

He came down beside her, straddling her body with powerful thighs, the revealing bulge of his erection tenting the suddenly tight crotch of his trousers. 'Demetri,' she breathed weakly, half in protest, and for an answer he bent and took one straining nipple into his mouth.

It was too much. Jane couldn't fight him any more. With Demetri suckling her breast, she was already throbbing with the need for him to touch her in other, wetter, places. She wanted to reach out and stroke him, to trace the line of soft hair that disappeared into his waistband. But when she reached for his zip, he stopped her.

'Soon, *agapi mou*,' he said, shifting back so he could unfasten his trousers and tug them off. 'Just not too soon, hmm?'

If he'd been wearing any underwear, it disappeared along with his trousers and Jane could see his manhood rearing proudly from its nest of dark hair. Then he parted her legs and lowered his head, laving her with his tongue until he had her twisting and turning beneath him.

'*Theos*, you taste so sweet,' he muttered thickly. 'Shall I make you come?'

'Not—not without you,' she said, her voice unsteady, yet not too wrapped up in her own needs not to know she wanted him inside her when she climaxed.

'*Iseh etimi,*' he groaned. Are you ready? And with one swift, hard lunge he thrust into her, his thick length stretching her and filling her so completely that she let out a breathless cry. Then, with his body hair brushing her thighs, he expelled a hoarse breath. 'You're so tight. Did I hurt you?'

'I'm OK,' she assured him huskily, her muscles quickening automatically about him. 'Just—just do it, Demetri. Don't—wait…'

As if he could, thought Demetri grimly. It was hard enough to control the urge he had to slam himself into her until it was done. Only the desire to savour the moment had him rocking back on his heels, looking down at the point where their bodies were joined so completely. However crazy this might be, he'd never wanted her more than he did right now.

'Demetri,' she protested weakly, and with a groan he pushed into her again. She closed about him, slick and tight, and the driving need for satisfaction blanked his mind.

'*Ineh ereos,*' he said thickly. You're beautiful. Then rocking back again, '*Theos,* I don't want this to end.'

'Me neither,' she confessed, but that didn't stop her from

lifting her legs to wind them about his hips. Then he felt the convulsion as she lost control and holding back became academic.

Her liquid heat drenched him, more than enough to send him over the edge. He moaned as the force of his release spilled from him. Shuddering with mindless pleasure, he emptied himself into her, and then slumped across her body in a total state of abandon.

Demetri opened his eyes to the sound of a shower running. For a moment he stared up at the ceiling above his head, seeing nothing familiar in its papered surface, sure he'd never seen a ceiling in that particular shade of peach before.

Then his eyes lowered to the windows, tall casement windows, shaded by ruched Roman blinds in a contrasting shade of lime green. The blinds were drawn against the daylight that was visible in a line above the sill.

Totally unfamiliar.

Yet suddenly totally recognisable.

Demetri sucked in a jagged breath, pushed himself into an upright position and looked about the room with unbelieving eyes. God, he was in Jane's apartment, Jane's bed! What in hell had he been thinking of? He'd come here to ask her for a divorce, not to have sex with her, for pity's sake.

He closed his eyes again, hoping against hope that it was all some crazy dream, that when he opened them again he'd be back in his own bedroom in Kalithi, with the sound of the Mediterranean a gentle murmur in his ears.

But it wasn't to be. When he lifted his lids for a second time, it was to find he was still occupying Jane's bed, a single sheet, which he suspected she'd thrown over him, covering him from hip to thigh.

Which was just as well, he reflected, conscious that an

awareness of his surroundings had done nothing to quell an arousal that was as vigorous as it was inappropriate. *Hristo*, he was supposed to be thinking of a way to get out of this with his dignity intact, not allowing his mind to wander into the bathroom and the delights of sharing Jane's shower.

Forcing himself to get out of bed, he groped for his boxers and pulled them on. Then, without giving himself time to think, he tugged his T-shirt over his head and stepped into his trousers, only cursing when he hurt himself fastening his zip.

The shower ceased abruptly, and, although he was tempted to wait and see what she'd be wearing when she came out of the bathroom, common sense had him snatching up his shoes and jacket and letting himself out of the bedroom before he made another mistake.

In the living room, he pushed his feet into his loafers and pulled on his jacket. Then he combed slightly unsteady fingers through his hair. *Theos,* he thought, looking about him, how had it happened? How had a simple conversation turned into a sensual assault on his senses?

Why had he been fool enough to go in there? Why hadn't he waited until she'd composed herself and then completed the interview with speed and objectivity? It was what she'd said she wanted, for heaven's sake. And when she'd first quit the room, he'd assumed she'd gone to get dressed and nothing else. It was only as the minutes had slipped by and there'd been no sound from the bedroom that he'd become suspicious.

Anxious, even, he conceded wryly. Jane had always been able to do that to him. In the three years they'd been together, he'd lost count of the number of occasions when she'd walked out on him. The fact was, he'd usually gone after her, desperate to assure himself that she was all right. Just like today.

He sighed. Even so, finding her in tears like that shouldn't have affected him as much as it had. It wasn't his fault they weren't still together, and if him asking for a divorce meant that much to her, why hadn't she tried to see him again before the situation had deteriorated as badly as it had?

None of it made any sense, not least the pleasure he'd gained from making love to her just now. He hated to admit it, but he hadn't enjoyed himself so much since the last time they'd been together.

Having sex with other women had never done it for him. And, although when Jane had left him he'd told himself it would be easy enough to replace her, he never had. He'd lost count of the number of women his mother had paraded in front of him, hoping to persuade him that remaining single wasn't an option for him. But his marriage to Jane had spoiled him for other woman, and he'd begun to believe that whatever happened he would never have that kind of sexual satisfaction again.

But now he had.

With her!

Although he'd sat down on the sofa to put on his shoes, now he got to his feet again. He couldn't sit still, not when his whole world was in turmoil. This was supposed to have been a short meeting, the courtesy of telling her himself instead of allowing her to learn the truth from his London solicitor. Instead, as his mother had feared, he'd allowed her to get under his skin, again.

He paced across to the windows, peering out at his limousine, parked at the front of the house. The chauffeur, who worked for Souvakis International, would be wondering what he was doing. But he knew better than to make any comments to his employer or anyone else.

The sound of a door opening behind him had him swinging round almost guiltily. Another sensation that was new to him. It occurred to him then that perhaps he ought to have left before she'd finished her shower. In spite of the fact that they hadn't finished their discussion, it could have waited until tomorrow or the next day. Now it was too late.

Jane came into the room rather tentatively. She'd taken the time to dry and straighten her hair and now it hung silky smooth to her shoulders. She'd put on a dark green T-shirt that clung to her breasts, and low-rise jeans exposed a delicate wedge of creamy pale skin.

She looked just as good to him now as she'd done before, thought Demetri grimly. If he hadn't known better, he'd have wondered if she'd worn the outfit deliberately to emphasise her eyes. She certainly looked tantalising, but her expression wasn't encouraging. Her eyes were guarded, cold, watching him with a wariness that bordered on contempt.

'You're still here,' she said, when he didn't speak. Then, making her way across the room, 'D'you want coffee?'

Coffee?

Demetri didn't know whether to be relieved or insulted. Only minutes before she'd been writhing beneath him, and now she was offering him coffee, as if they'd just been passing the time of day instead of having hot, sweaty sex.

'*Efkharisto, then thelo.*' Not for me, thank you. Demetri spoke tersely, following her across the room to where a small counter separated an equally small service kitchen from the rest of the room. He hesitated, and then added unwillingly, 'You are OK?'

Jane turned from filling a filter with coffee. 'Why wouldn't I be?' she countered, though this time he noticed she broke their gaze. 'Go and sit down. I won't be long.'

'I'd rather not.' Demetri took a deep breath. 'Are we going to talk about this?'

Jane concentrated on setting the jug on the hotplate. Then,

when it was placed to her satisfaction, she opened a cupboard above her head and took down a porcelain mug. Glancing fleetingly in his direction, the mug in her hand, she said, 'Are you sure you don't want anything to drink?'

'I'm sure.' Demetri could feel impatience digging away at his good nature. What the hell was she trying to do? Pretend it had never happened? 'Jane, look at me,' he said sharply. 'No, not like that. Really look at me. What are you thinking? Tell me!'

CHAPTER THREE

JANE found it impossible to do as he asked. OK, she knew that nothing had changed really. Just because they'd had sex— pretty phenomenal sex, as it happened—didn't make a scrap of difference to Demetri. Sex was what he did. Particularly when he wanted something from her. It had always been a damn good means of getting his own way in the past. And he must be thinking she was such a pushover. He'd only had to tumble her onto the bed and she'd been practically begging him to do it.

She'd been so stupid, she thought bitterly. If only he hadn't chosen to come here at a time when she was not only exhausted from her trip, but expecting her period as well. She was always overly emotional at this time of the month. And his deliberate kindness had been the last straw.

'I'm not thinking anything,' she lied now, as the water dripped through the filter. Then, turning the tables, 'What about you? What are you thinking, Demetri?'

Believe me, you don't want to know, Demetri reflected drily, aware that his thoughts ran along the lines of taking her back to bed. But he'd be crazy to admit that. It would expose a weakness and he was already feeling far too exposed as it was.

'I'm thinking—I should apologise,' he declared at last,

choosing the least provocative option. 'I—never intended this to happen.'

'Well, that makes two of us,' said Jane at once and Demetri felt a fist twisting in his gut. Did she have to sound so dismissive? Couldn't she at least have admitted that she'd been partially to blame?

But that wasn't going to happen, he realised, and, leaving the counter, he walked back to the position he'd previously occupied beside the window. His limousine still stood there and he wished he could just get into the car and drive away. He wanted to forget what had happened, forget that when he'd come here he'd been looking for closure. Closure! His lips twisted. Instead, he'd torn away a veneer and left what felt like an open wound.

'So?' He heard her voice and turned to find Jane had come to perch on the arm of one of the sofas. She was holding a mug filled with black coffee and she lifted enquiring eyes to his face. 'Do I take it there's someone else?'

It was such a ludicrous question in the circumstances. Demetri was tempted to say 'Damn you!' and walk out. He felt so foolish having to admit that that was the reason he'd come here. That he was intending to marry someone else when he was free.

But he didn't have a choice in the matter. It was what was expected of him as his father's eldest son. When Leonidas Souvakis retired, he'd handed the control of Souvakis International to him. And such power held responsibilities, not all of them to do with the company itself.

'My father's dying,' he said at last, deciding he didn't owe her any consideration. But even so, he was unprepared for the way the colour drained out of her face.

'Leo is dying?' she echoed faintly. 'My God, why didn't you tell me?' Her soft lips parted in mute denial. 'I can't believe it. He was so—so fit; so strong.'

'Cancer is no respecter of strength or otherwise,' responded Demetri flatly. 'He found a lump. He did nothing about it. He said he was too busy.' He shrugged. 'When he did go and see the doctor, it was too late to operate.'

'Oh, God!' Jane put down her cup and pressed both hands to her cheeks. Her eyes were once again filled with tears. 'Poor Leo. He's such a good man, a kind man. He was always kind to me. He made me welcome when your mother never did.'

Demetri said nothing. He knew that what she'd said was true. His mother had never wanted him to marry an English girl. Their values were so different, she'd insisted. And ultimately she'd been proved to be right.

Now Jane attempted to pull herself together. 'How long have you known?' she asked, wondering what this had to do with Demetri wanting a divorce. She paused, trying to find a connection. 'Does he want to see me?'

Demetri was taken aback. Although he had no doubt that Leo Souvakis would have liked to see his daughter-in-law again, his mother would never agree to it. For the past five years she'd persistently begged her son to go and see a priest and try to arrange an annulment of his marriage to Jane. She was sure Father Panaystakis would do everything in his power to get some special dispensation from the church.

But, ironically, Demetri had been in no hurry to sever his relationship. It had been convenient in all sorts of ways. Not least to discourage any gold-digging female from getting the wrong idea. Now remaining unattached was no longer an option and only a divorce would do.

His silence must have given Jane her answer, however, because now she said, 'Then I don't understand. What does your father's illness have to do with you asking for a divorce?'

Demetri's sigh was heavy. He pushed his balled fists into his trouser pockets and rocked back on his heels before he spoke. '*Mi pateras*—my father,' he corrected himself, 'wants a grandchild. Grand*children*. With Yanis a priest and Stefan not interested in women, the responsibility falls to me.'

'How archaic!' Jane was sardonic. Then she frowned. 'But what about—' she hesitated '—the boy?'

'Ianthe's son?' Demetri was matter-of-fact, and Jane's nails dug into her palms. 'Marc died. I thought you knew.'

Jane was incensed. 'And you thought this, why? We haven't exactly kept in touch, Demetri.'

He shrugged as if acknowledging her words. '*Poli kala*, Marc caught pneumonia when he was only a few days old.' His voice was tight. 'The doctors tried to save him, but he was too small, too premature. He didn't stand a chance.'

Jane caught her breath. 'Poor Ianthe,' she said, finding she meant it.

'*Neh*, poor Ianthe,' echoed Demetri, though there was a distinct edge of bitterness to his tone. 'She didn't deserve that.'

'No.' Jane shook her head, reaching for her coffee again. She took a gulp, grateful for the rush of caffeine. 'So now I suppose you two are planning on getting married at last.' She tried to sound casual. 'Your mother will be pleased.'

Demetri's thin—yet oh, so sensual—lips curled into a scowl. 'No,' he told her harshly. 'I was never interested in Ianthe, despite what you believed. I intend to marry Ariadne Pavlos. You may remember the Pavlos family. Ariadne and I have been friends since we were children. She has recently returned from an extended visit to the United States.'

'How nice!' Jane tried not to let her true feelings show. Ariadne's mother, Sofia Pavlos, was a friend of Demetri's mother, she remembered. Someone else who hadn't approved of their marriage. She moistened her lips. 'Does Ariadne know about Ianthe's baby, too?'

'She knows enough,' said Demetri shortly, realising he was getting into deep water. The past was the past and there was no point in raking it all up now. He shouldn't have come here. He should have taken his lawyer's advice and let him handle it. But he hadn't realised how dangerous it would be for him to get involved with Jane again.

'Look,' he said, when the silence had become unbearable, 'I've got to get going.' He sucked in a breath before adding, 'I'm sure you hate me now, but I really didn't intend to—to—'

'Seduce me?'

'No.' Demetri was angry. 'It was hardly a seduction. You met me halfway.'

Jane's colour deepened. 'All right. Perhaps that was unjustified. But it wouldn't be the first time you used—it—against me.'

Demetri swore then. 'What do you expect me to say, Jane? I came here to warn you about the divorce, that's all. I didn't expect to find you half-naked.'

Jane gasped. 'What?' she choked. 'I'm so irresistible I got under your guard?'

'Something like that,' muttered Demetri, aware that he wasn't doing himself any favours. He straightened and moved towards the door. 'I'll have my lawyer contact you with all the details. Despite—well, despite your attitude, I won't contest any settlement your lawyer asks for.'

Jane sprang up from the sofa, almost spilling her coffee in the process. 'I've told you, I don't want any of your money, Demetri!' she exclaimed angrily. 'I'm quite capable of supporting myself, thank you.'

'*Ala—*'

'Forget it!' Without giving him any further time to defend

himself, she strode towards the outer door and jerked it open. 'Get out of here, Demetri. Before I say something I'll regret.'

Demetri flew back to Kalithi that afternoon.

He had planned to stay a couple more days. He'd been invited to attend a meeting of the Association of Oil Producers the following morning, but he'd had his assistant call and offer his apologies instead. His father wouldn't be pleased. He'd been delighted that the Souvakis Corporation had garnered such respect in the oil-producing countries, and it had also proved he had been judicious in handing control of the organisation to his son.

Demetri wasn't so sure, however. He'd already realised that being head of an organisation like Souvakis International demanded a considerable amount of his time. It might even be said that the responsibilities he'd taken on eight years ago had played no small part in the breakdown of his marriage. If he and Jane had had more time to talk about what had happened, more time for him to persuade her he was innocent of the charge she'd levelled against him, she might not have walked out as she did. But she'd believed that he was to blame for Ianthe's pregnancy, and without proof he'd been unable to convince her otherwise.

It was already dark when the powerful little Cessna landed on the island. The airstrip was a private one, owned by the Souvakis family, and although the island attracted tourists, they came by ferry, landing at the small port of Kalithi in the south of the island.

Headlights scanning the runway were an indication that his father had got the message he'd sent earlier, though he guessed the old man would want to know exactly why he had avoided speaking to him personally.

His own personal assistant, Theo Vasilis, had travelled with him, and it was he who was first off the plane, organising the transport that would take them to the Souvakis estate. A sleek four-wheel-drive vehicle stood at the edge of the tarmac, waiting for the preliminaries of landing to be over. Then, when Demetri strode across the apron to get into it, he discovered it wasn't his father's chauffeur who was driving. Ariadne Pavlos was seated behind the wheel, her glossy lips parted in a smile that was both welcoming and slightly smug.

'*Eh,*' she said, when Demetri climbed into the vehicle beside her. 'A nice surprise, no?'

Demetri's jaw tightened momentarily, the knowledge that he would have preferred not to have to deal with Ariadne tonight giving him pause. But then, realising why he was feeling this way, he forced a smile and leant across the console to kiss her. 'A very nice surprise,' he said untruthfully. 'Have you been waiting long?'

'Only about six years,' she responded artfully, her tongue making contact with his before he could pull away. 'You have missed me, yes?'

Demetri turned to fasten his seat belt. 'What do you think?' he asked, avoiding a direct reply. Then, in an effort to change the subject, 'How is my father? Not too pleased that I cut the oil conference, I'll bet.'

'He is—OK.' Ariadne spoke indifferently, glancing round with some impatience when Theo Vasilis deposited their luggage rather heavily into the back of the car. '*Prosekheh*!' she exclaimed irritably. Be careful. Then her eyes widened even further when Theo swung open the rear door and climbed into the back. Her head swung round to Demetri. 'Must he come with us?'

'Why not?' Demetri's response was innocent enough, but he couldn't deny a sense of relief that Theo was coming along. He nodded towards the laptop the other man was carrying. 'My father will expect a report on the meetings we've had while we've been in London.'

'The meetings with your wife?' suggested Ariadne silkily, her dark eyes alight with malice. 'Oh, yes. I will be interested to hear about those myself.'

Demetri expelled a long breath. 'Not that meeting,' he said flatly. 'The meetings we had with business associates.'

'Ah, but those meetings are so boring, no?' said Ariadne archly. 'Tell me about your wife. Is she going to be difficult, do you think?'

Difficult! Demetri stifled the groan of frustration that rose inside him. But, 'Not difficult, no,' he told her, and then turned again to Theo in the back seat. 'Did you collect all the papers from the plane?'

His meaning couldn't have been plainer and, although Ariadne tossed her head as she reached for the ignition, she knew better than to pursue the matter now. There'd be time enough later, Demetri could almost hear her thinking. And dammit, why not? It was because of her—and his father's illness—that he'd gone to see Jane in the first place.

Leaving the airport behind, they drove along the narrow country lane that led to the Souvakis estate. There was little to see in the car's headlights but the coarse grass that grew alongside the road and the occasional stunted cypress. But Demetri knew that running parallel with the track were the sand dunes and beyond that the blue-green waters of the Aegean. It was spring in the islands and it would be good to wake up tomorrow morning and hear the murmur of the ocean instead of the hum of traffic outside his window.

But thinking of London wasn't the wisest thing to do in the circumstances. It reminded him too much of what had happened earlier in the day. And he couldn't help but compare Ariadne's dark, somewhat sultry, good looks with his wife's fair-skinned beauty. They were so different, he thought, not welcoming the comparison: Ariadne, full-figured and voluptuous, and Jane, tall, slender, hiding her sensuous nature behind a tantalising façade of cool composure.

He squashed that thought, saying tersely, 'Did you attend your cousin's wedding?'

'Julia? But, of course.' Ariadne shrugged as the tall wooden gates that marked the entrance to the estate came into view. She flashed the car's headlights, and a man appeared from the white-painted gatehouse to one side of the gates, hurriedly releasing the latch and throwing them wide. 'Naturally, I was the only woman there without an escort. Thia Thermia said I should not have allowed you to go away at such a time.'

'She would.' Demetri's mouth compressed. He wasn't unduly worried what Thermia Adonides thought of him. She was also Ianthe's mother and because of that she already disapproved of him. He'd been amazed that she hadn't attempted to thwart his and Ariadne's relationship, but evidently the advantages of his wealth far outweighed any misgivings she might retain.

Demetri raised a hand to Georgiou, the gatekeeper, as they drove past, and then the powerful vehicle was accelerating up the long, winding drive to the main house. The villa, which stood on a small plateau overlooking the ocean, was still occupied by his parents. Demetri had built his own house on the property, but since Jane's departure he tended to spend much of his time elsewhere.

His mother often complained that they saw little of him, and it was true that until his father's illness, Demetri had spent little time at home. He worked hard, and there was no denying that his work had saved his sanity. If he'd played hard, too, he'd told himself he deserved it. He'd been certain he'd never succumb to any other woman's appeal.

And he hadn't. It was only when he'd discovered his father's illness was terminal that he'd been persuaded to consider marrying again. Ariadne was the perfect candidate: she was single, she was Greek and his mother approved of her.

A paved forecourt fronted the cluster of buildings that comprised barns and garages as well as his parents' home. Ariadne brought the car to a halt and turned off the engine. But when Theo sprang out and Demetri made to open his door, her hand on his arm arrested him.

'Wait,' she said huskily. 'Talk to me, Demetri. Tell me you haven't changed your mind.'

Demetri stared at her, the lights that encircled the courtyard illuminating the anxious expression in her dark eyes. 'Changed my mind?' he echoed, suddenly feeling horribly guilty. He put out his hand and cupped her cheek. 'Sweetheart, whatever gave you that idea?'

CHAPTER FOUR

WELL, she was pregnant.

Trying to think pragmatically, Jane took a deep breath and pushed the cartridge she'd been examining back into her bag. It was the third positive reaction she'd had in the last two weeks, and, however much she tried to persuade herself that these tests could be faulty, even she didn't believe it could happen three times in a row.

Dammit!

Smudging back a tear, she sniffed ferociously. How could it have happened? She'd been so sure that when she and Demetri had made—had had sex, she amended, fiercely, her monthly cycle had been too far along for her to conceive. She'd always been so regular in the past. Though she had to admit that when they were living together, she hadn't left anything to chance.

In the beginning, they'd both agreed that having children could wait. For a year or two, at least. And because Jane wanted to go on working, Demetri had opened a small gallery for her in the town of Kalithi itself. It had meant that she'd been able to keep in contact with Olga, who'd been happy to exchange antiquities and paintings with her erstwhile student.

It had all worked very well, and because she owned the

gallery Jane had been able to accompany Demetri on his business trips whenever she chose. It had seemed an idyllic existence, and she'd never been happier.

But then Ianthe had revealed she was pregnant, and her whole house of cards had come tumbling down about her ears. Jane hadn't been able to forgive Demetri for betraying her, her only relief in the knowledge that they had no children to suffer the break-up of their parents' marriage.

She sighed. If she was honest, she'd have to admit that taking precautions hadn't figured too highly in her thoughts when Demetri had kissed her. The sensual brush of his tongue had banished all other thoughts from her head. She'd wanted him, she acknowledged, just as much as he'd wanted her. It had been far too easy to convince herself that he wasn't just using her for his own ends.

It wasn't until two weeks later, when she still hadn't had her period, that she'd even considered the alternative. And even then it had been hard to believe that that reckless consummation had had such a result. It was five weeks now since Demetri had come to her apartment. She'd already received notification that he'd contacted his solicitors about the divorce. Dear God, what was she going to do?

The appearance of her employer forced her to shelve the problem for the moment. Although Olga Ivanovitch was almost seventy, she strode into Jane's office at the gallery with all the vitality of a much younger woman. A Russian Jew, whose parents had been living in Germany just before the last war, she and her family had fled to England. It was her father who'd founded the gallery, but Olga who had made it a success, moving the premises from Croyden to their present enviable position in the West End.

In long skirts and with a cloak floating freely about her tall generous figure, she looked a little like an ageing flower-child, Jane thought. But Olga had been her mentor, taking her on when all Jane had to commend her was a degree in fine arts from a redbrick university and an enthusiasm Olga had recognised that matched her own.

Now Olga brushed back her mane of incongruously red hair and said impatiently, 'Did he come?' And, although she'd lived in England long enough to have mastered the language completely, her accent still remained for artistic effect.

'He came,' agreed Jane, knowing at once who Olga was talking about. A famous collector of antiquities had expressed an interest in the set of bronzes Jane had brought back from Bangkok. He'd promised to call at the gallery that morning to examine them again and make his decision.

'And?' Olga couldn't hide her excitement.

'He bought them,' Jane responded drily. 'He wants them packed and delivered by courier to his home in Suffolk.'

'Wonderful!' Olga was delighted. 'And a healthy commission for you, too, *leibchen*. You have done well. I must send you away again. You have the knack for finding treasure in the most unexpected places.'

Jane managed a small smile, but inside she felt chewed-up, unable to think of anything but the cartridge she'd hidden in her bag. Her hand stole disbelievingly over her flat stomach. Was it possible that Demetri's baby was already growing inside her? How soon would it be before it became noticeable? How soon before Olga suspected that something was wrong?

And, as if she'd already sensed her employee's abstraction, Olga rested a hip on Jane's desk. 'You are looking pale,' she said, dark brows drawing together above her long nose. 'Are you getting enough sleep? Or is that young man of yours keeping you up half the night, hmm?'

Jane shuffled the papers on her desk. 'I don't have a young man, Olga. I've told you so a dozen times. Alex Hunter and I are just friends.'

'Does he know that?'

Predictably, now that the news of the bronzes was out of the way, Olga was directing all her attention towards her assistant. How would she react when she found out Jane was having a baby? How would Alex react when she'd already assured him that her relationship with Demetri was over?

Playing for time, she said weakly, 'I beg your pardon—'

'Mr Hunter,' said Olga testily. 'I was asking if he was aware that you have nothing more than friendship in mind?'

'Oh…' Jane made a helpless gesture. 'Our relationship isn't that serious. I like Alex. He's good company. But we've only known one another for a comparatively short time.'

'Long enough.' Olga was persistent. 'I worry about you, Jane, I really do. When are you going to put the past behind you and get on with your life?'

'Oh, I—'

Jane was still trying to think of an answer when Olga spoke again. 'Isn't it time you thought about getting a divorce?'

Sometimes Olga's perception was truly startling, Jane thought incredulously. At any other time, she might have admired her ability to sense what she was thinking. But not today. This was one occasion when Jane would prefer to keep her thoughts to herself.

While she waited for Jane to answer, Olga rummaged in her pocket and drew out a pack of her favourite Gauloise cigarettes. Placing one between her lips, she flicked her lighter, inhaling deeply before blowing a stream of blue smoke into the air above their heads. Jane had never liked the smell of cigarettes and this morning she found it nauseating. Feeling the bile rising in her throat, she made an incoherent little sound and then rushed wildly out of the room.

In the small bathroom that adjoined the gallery, she was violently sick. Leaning against the tiled wall afterwards, a tissue pressed to her mouth, she thought it was a long time since she'd felt so ill. What had she eaten, for God's sake? She'd only had toast for breakfast, so it couldn't be that. Mind you, she hadn't really wanted any breakfast. She'd been feeling distinctly out-of-sorts since she'd got out of bed.

And then, feeling immensely stupid, she realised what was happening. It wasn't food-poisoning. It wasn't even the smell of Olga's cigarette, although heaven knew they were an acquired taste. No, this had to be the start of morning sickness, and if she needed any further confirmation of her condition, this was it.

A tentative tapping at the door roused her. 'Jane? Jane, are you all right?' Naturally, it was Olga. 'Is something wrong?'

Everything, thought Jane heavily, struggling to pull herself together. But she managed to say, 'No, I'm OK, Olga. I think I must have eaten something that disagreed with me and when I smelled your cigarette—'

'*Mein Gott!*' Olga sounded horrified. 'My cigarette has made you ill?'

'No. No, not really.' Jane felt ashamed. She couldn't let Olga take the blame for something that was her own fault. She opened the door to find the old woman waiting outside, wringing her hands anxiously. 'Sorry about that.'

Olga said something Jane couldn't understand and then wrapped her arm about the younger woman's shoulders. Thankfully, she'd ditched the cigarette but Jane could still smell the scent of tobacco on her clothes.

'*Liebchen,*' she murmured with evident concern. 'Are you sure you and Mr Hunter are just good friends?'

'What do you mean?' Jane tried to sound confused but it didn't quite come off.

Olga sighed, looking down at her with considering eyes. 'Because…well, because I am wondering if there might be another reason for you feeling—unwell, no?'

'Another reason?' Jane swallowed.

'Do I have to draw you a picture, *leibling*?' Olga turned to take her by the shoulders, making it impossible for Jane to avoid her calculating stare. 'Is it possible that you might—be fooling yourself?'

'Fooling myself?' Jane blew out a breath, wondering if it was worth pretending she didn't understand. Giving in, she said, 'Are you suggesting I might be pregnant? Is that what you think?'

Olga shook her head. 'I'm simply saying it's a possibility you should consider, no? You wouldn't be the first young woman to fall for the charms of a handsome young man like Mr Hunter.'

Jane pulled away from her. 'I've told you!' she exclaimed fiercely. 'Alex and I—Alex and I have never—'

'Never?' Olga was sceptical.

'Never,' retorted Jane crossly. 'Now, can we talk about something else?' She scrubbed at her mouth one last time and then started back towards her office. 'Have you given any thought as to where we might find the other pieces Sir George is looking for?'

Olga shrugged, following her more slowly, and Jane knew the old woman still wasn't convinced of her answer. However, until she'd decided what she was going to do, Jane didn't feel capable of discussing her situation with anyone. For heaven's sake, she still hadn't come to terms with the fact that she was pregnant herself.

But, throughout the rest of the day, Jane found her thoughts constantly drifting to the dilemma she was facing. What was she going to do? How soon would she have to decide whether she was going to keep the baby or not? For, although her salary was generous, there was no way she could afford the cost of child-care in London on her own.

The alternative was to tell Demetri about the baby. But how could she tell her husband she was expecting a baby when he was already preparing to get a divorce? And there were other people involved, not least the woman he hoped to marry. As well as his mother. Jane could well imagine Maria Souvakis's reaction when she discovered her son had fathered another child. With the despised English girl.

Jane packed up early and left for home, telling Olga she was feeling shivery. She hoped mentioning another ailment would divert her employer's mind from the suspicions she'd voiced earlier. But feeling the woman's eyes upon her as she ran down the steps from the gallery, Jane wasn't confident she'd succeeded.

It was raining and she took the bus home, afraid that if she took the underground the smell of cigarette smoke would make her sick again. And it was such a relief to walk into the quiet, airy spaciousness of her apartment, so good to sink down onto the sofa with a freshly-made cup of tea.

However, she hadn't been sitting there for very long before the phone rang. Her mother, Jane guessed, assuming that she'd phoned the gallery and Olga had directed her here. It was to be hoped her employer hadn't decided to confide her fears to Mrs Lang. It might account for the timeliness—or untimeliness—of her call.

She contemplated not answering for all of ten seconds. But the possibility that it might be someone else had her reaching for the receiver. 'Yes,' she said, aware that her tone was less than cordial, and then she nearly dropped the instrument when Demetri's rich, dark voice came on the line.

'I see your temper hasn't improved,' he remarked drily, the slight echo indicating he was calling long-distance. 'Who has upset you this time?'

Jane caught her breath. Then, gathering her scattered senses, she said, 'Nobody's upset me, Demetri. I haven't spoken to you in weeks.'

Demetri snorted. 'Always ready with the acid comment,' he said wryly. 'I suppose you were expecting me to call.'

Jane frowned. 'Why would I expect to hear from you?' she retorted, wondering if there was a letter in today's mail she'd overlooked. This had to be something to do with the divorce. There was no other reason for Demetri to contact her. That *he* knew of, at least.

'I spoke to your mother earlier,' Demetri explained with more patience than she'd have expected. 'I didn't have the gallery's number so I was forced to contact her. She gave me the number—not without some reluctance, I have to admit— but, as you know, the effort was wasted. You're an elusive woman, Jane.' He paused. 'I trust you're feeling better.'

Jane moistened her lips. Despite the fact that her mind was buzzing with the reasons why Demetri had rung, she wondered rather apprehensively what Olga might have said. Nothing indiscreet, she assured herself, although Olga wasn't known for her discretion.

'Um—I suppose Olga told you I'd gone home because I wasn't feeling well,' she ventured cautiously.

'Something like that,' Demetri agreed obliquely. 'I hope it's nothing serious.'

Serious enough, thought Jane tensely, but Demetri hadn't rung to discuss her health. 'Just a cold,' she said, realising she had to move the conversation along. 'What did you want, Demetri?' A thought occurred to her. 'Your father's not worse, is he?'

'No.' Demetri was upbeat. 'As a matter of fact, he seems a little better. The drugs his doctors have prescribed seem to be keeping the tumour in check.'

'Oh, I'm so glad.' Jane was fervent. 'Give him my best wishes when you see him, won't you? I've thought about him a lot.'

'Really?'

'Yes, really.' Jane was stung by the trace of disbelief in his voice. 'Just because a man takes what he wants without care of the consequences doesn't mean his father deserves my contempt.'

She heard his angry intake of breath. 'You're still talking about Ianthe, I presume,' he said harshly.

Jane swallowed. 'What else?'

'Oh, I don't know.' Demetri's tone was sardonic now. 'I thought it might have been your less-than-subtle way of remind-ing me of what happened when I came to your apartment.'

Jane's fingers tightened round the receiver. 'Do you need reminding?'

Demetri swore. 'It was good, Jane, but it wasn't that good. If you think that's what I want to talk to you about, you're wasting your time provoking me.'

Jane gasped. 'You—you—'

'Bastard? Son of a bitch?' supplied Demetri coldly. 'Yes, I know what you think of me, Jane. You don't have to spell it out.'

'Then why are you ringing me?' she demanded. 'If it's not to apologise, I don't think I want to hear anything you have to say.'

She would have rung off then, but his hoarse 'Wait!' caused her to hesitate in the act. 'My father—my father wants to see you,' he went on grimly. 'Don't ask me why, but he does.' He sucked in a breath. 'Will you come?'

Jane was stunned. 'To Greece?'

'To Kalithi, of course.'

Jane couldn't believe it. 'You're not serious!'

'Why not?' Demetri had himself in control again. 'He would deem it a great personal favour if you would accept his invitation.'

'But…' There were so many 'buts' Jane couldn't even begin to think of them all. 'Your mother would never agree to it—'

'She has no choice.'

'—and you don't want me there—'

'That's immaterial.'

'Besides, I can't just leave my job. Olga depends on me.'

'Take a leave of absence,' said Demetri tersely. 'If it's the money you're concerned about—'

'It's not.' Jane resented his immediate supposition that money could solve everything.

'Then I don't see the problem.' He paused. 'Unless you think your boyfriend won't approve of it. You didn't tell me you had a boyfriend, Jane. How long has this been going on?'

Jane caught her breath. She was tempted to say 'It's none of your business', but in this case it was wiser not to lie. 'Alex Hunter is a friend, that's all. Not a *boy*friend. I assume Olga told you about him.' That was like her. 'Well, she's very keen for me to find someone to care about me.'

'And does he?' enquired Demetri, startling her into confusion.

'Does he what?'

'Care about you,' Demetri declared smoothly. 'Your employer tells me he's an accountant, with a very good job in the City. I have to say, I can't see you with an accountant, *aghapita*. Grey men in grey suits—isn't that what they say, *okhi*?'

'Whom I choose to see is nothing to do with you.' Jane was forced to defend Alex, regardless. She took a breath. 'You really expect me to accept your father's invitation?' she continued incredulously. She shook her head. 'Why does he want to see me? Do you know?'

'Perhaps he wants to say goodbye.' Demetri's tone was

sombre. 'I hope you will put our differences aside for the few days you will be staying at the villa. It's not as if it was ever your home. The house I built for us is some distance from the main building, as you know. If you'd prefer it, I'll keep out of your way.'

CHAPTER FIVE

IT WAS late afternoon when the ferry docked at Kalithi. It had been a three-hour journey from Andros, where Jane's flight from England had landed, and by the time she stepped ashore she was feeling decidedly weary.

It was already a week since Demetri's call and five days since a doctor had confirmed her condition. She still hadn't told anyone she was pregnant, despite the fact that the morning sickness hadn't abated, and she knew Olga wasn't deceived when Jane insisted it was just a bug.

Mrs Lang, whom she'd had to tell where she was going, had assumed her daughter's anxious appearance was apprehension about seeing the Souvakis family again. In her opinion, Jane should have refused the invitation, despite its poignant cause. It was ridiculous, she said, as Jane and Demetri were in the process of getting divorced.

Olga had been of a like mind. Knowing nothing of Demetri's visit to Jane's apartment, she naturally believed that, if Jane was pregnant, Alex Hunter was to blame. The young accountant, who worked for the firm who audited Olga's books, thankfully knew nothing of her suspicions, and like Olga he'd been totally against this trip.

'It seems funny to me that just weeks after informing you

that he wants a divorce, he suggests you go out there to see his father!' he'd exclaimed when Jane phoned to explain why she wouldn't be able to see him for a few days. 'Do you trust him? Are you sure this isn't just a ploy to get you back?'

'Oh, please!' At the end of an exhausting day Jane had found it hard to keep her patience. She'd already had a similar discussion with Olga, who wasn't at all pleased that her assistant was taking a week's unplanned-for leave. 'Demetri wants a divorce. I've told you that. But—well, his father is very ill. He says he wants to see me.'

'He *says*.' Alex had pounced on the word. 'So you've only his say-so that Leonides Souvakis is ill?'

'Demetri wouldn't lie about something like that,' Jane had replied firmly, wondering why she felt so sure about it when Demetri had lied to her before. 'Besides which, he's already got a girlfriend. A Greek girl. He intends to marry her as soon as he's free.'

'I see.'

Alex had been somewhat mollified by her answer, but Jane had wondered if Olga might not be right in thinking he had more than a platonic friendship in mind. A friend wouldn't have interrogated her, wouldn't have behaved as if he had some right to question her movements. And when he'd asked how long she planned to stay in Greece, she'd been deliberately vague.

Now, stepping onto Greek soil again, she wondered if she had been wise in coming here. How was she going to feel, seeing Demetri again and knowing she was carrying his baby? For whatever he'd said, she was fairly sure she would see him. It would be totally out of character for him to neglect his parents just because he thought she'd prefer him to stay away.

Jane only had one bag, a bulky haversack that she could loop over her shoulder, but she was still one of the last to step ashore.

There was no sign of Demetri, but she couldn't help feeling wary. She knew it was twenty minutes' drive from the small port to the Souvakis estate and she didn't remember ever seeing a taxi. Or needing one, she reflected, remembering the sleek little sports car Demetri had given her to get about the island.

She was hovering beside the pile of produce that was being unloaded from the ferry when she saw a woman watching her. She didn't think she'd seen her before, yet there was something vaguely familiar about her. Of medium height, with strong, exotic features, she was typical of many Greek women Jane had seen in the past. But her clothes and the way she held herself set her apart and Jane felt her heartbeat quicken when she started towards her.

'Are you Jane?' she asked, her accent making the words difficult to understand. Or perhaps it was the almost scornful way she spoke Jane's name that made the difference. And the fact that, although they were strangers, she hadn't used her surname.

And, because Jane was feeling tired and not altogether friendly, she replied, 'That's right. Have you been sent to meet me?'

The woman surveyed her thoroughly before responding and Jane was instantly conscious that the short-sleeved T-shirt, cropped linen trousers and canvas boots she'd worn to travel in suffered by comparison to a silk vest, a flaring peasant-style skirt and high heels. 'I have *come* to meet you,' the woman corrected her. 'Kiria Souvakis thought it would be a good idea for us to get to know one another, *neh?* I am Ariadne Pavlos. Demetri and I are to be married when he is free of his marriage to you.'

Jane was taken aback, although she had to admit it was typical of Demetri's mother to pull a stunt like this. Sending Demetri's—what?—his new girlfriend…his future fiancée? His *lover* to meet her was a little brutal even for Maria. She wondered if Demetri knew of it. She supposed he had to. Little went on here without his being aware of it.

'How nice,' she said now, refusing to let Ariadne see that she'd disturbed her. She glanced about her. 'Do you have a car?'

'*Veveha.*' Of course. Ariadne had clearly not expected Jane to take it so calmly. 'It is over here. If you'll come?'

The car was painfully familiar. Ariadne was driving the dark red sports car Demetri had bought for her. Maria's doing again, Jane guessed, though Ariadne had to have gone along with it. She couldn't decide whether Demetri's mother was calculating or merely apprehensive.

Thankfully, the heat of the day was abating. It was late afternoon, and the island was bathed in a warm golden light. Summer came early to the Aegean, and, although much of the island was composed of rock and scrubland, here on the coastal plain flowers bloomed in ripe profusion.

Dumping her haversack into the back of the small car, Jane slid into the passenger seat beside Ariadne. '*Endaxi,*' the other woman declared tersely. OK. '*Pameh!*' Let's go.

If she thought Jane might not understand her, she was mistaken. Despite the fact that she'd only lived on Kalithi for a little over two years, Jane had managed to acquire a reasonable grasp of the language. She'd had to, to run her small gallery. And Demetri had liked her to speak to him in his own language, particularly when they were making love...

The memory was disturbing, particularly as she was sitting beside the girl who would soon be Demetri's wife. Unable to prevent herself, she ran a nervous hand over the slight swell of her stomach. Common sense told her she would have to tell Demetri about the baby. But the last thing she needed was for him to think she wanted him back.

'You are staying how long?'

Ariadne's question interrupted the uneasy direction of her thoughts, which was probably just as well, she told herself severely. She wasn't here because Demetri had invited her. It was his father who wanted to see her.

'I don't know,' she answered now, although she'd already booked her return flight for the end of the week. Her eyes drifted over the headland and the rugged cliffs that descended to the blue-green waters that lapped the shoreline. It was all so beautiful. She'd forgotten exactly how beautiful it was. 'How is Leo? Demetri said he was feeling a little better.'

Ariadne took her eyes off the winding road to glance at her. 'Kirieh Souvakis is —well,' she replied after a moment, 'a little—confused, *isos*. We have been very worried about him.'

'I'm sure.' Jane tried to feel sympathetic towards her. But she had the feeling Ariadne was more concerned about her being here than she was about Demetri's father. There was a certain lack of emotion in her words.

'*Veveha,* he is most anxious to see Demetri happy at last,' Ariadne continued, apparently unaware of speaking out of turn. Or, more likely, she didn't care what Jane thought of her. 'It is not good for a man to be without a wife and family.'

Jane's lips compressed. 'Demetri has a wife,' she couldn't resist saying, and Ariadne gave her another knowing look.

'Not for much longer, *sostos?*' she murmured silkily. 'Demetri tells me you are not going to make any trouble about the divorce.'

'Does he?' Jane was tempted to say he should have thought of that before he'd gone to bed with her, but it wasn't in her nature to be deliberately cruel. 'No, well, he's probably right.'

'Probably?' Ariadne latched on to the word.

Jane turned her head towards the ocean again. 'Where is Demetri? Back at the house?'

There was a petulant silence and then Ariadne said, with

evident reluctance, 'He's away. On business. He won't be back until the end of the week.'

Jane felt a pain twist inside her. But it wasn't a physical thing, merely an acknowledgement that, despite the fact that Demetri was doing as he'd said, she was devastated by the news. So, it looked as if she wasn't going to see him, after all. That should make her decision easier.

Or not.

'You were expecting to see him, were you not?'

Ariadne couldn't leave it alone, and Jane had to bite her tongue on the bitter response she could have given. 'You couldn't be more wrong,' she said, silencing the voice inside her that told quite a different story. 'Oh, we're almost there.'

It was all too painfully familiar. The wooden gates at the foot of the drive, the winding track, edged with trees that provided a perfect screen for the house. And then the villa itself, white-painted and expansive, black shutters open, orange tiles reflecting the late-afternoon sun.

Jane caught her breath. She couldn't help it, but she quickly disguised it beneath a sudden clearing of her throat. Just because she was assailed by memories was no reason to feel nostalgic. She'd left the island of her own accord, almost destroyed by her husband's deceit.

Ariadne brought the car to a halt and Jane thrust open her door and got out before the girl could say anything else. She hadn't asked to come here and she had no intention of mitigating Ariadne's fears. If she had doubts about Demetri, let her deal with them. Jane just wanted to do what was necessary and leave. Whatever 'necessary' was.

A manservant appeared as Jane was reaching for her haversack, and she was quite willing to hand over the task to him. All the same, now that she was here, she was uncomfortably

aware of the absurdity of her position, and she hoped she would
be shown to her room and given time to compose herself before
meeting Demetri's parents again.

'*Apo etho ineh, kiria,*' the man said after he had hefted her
bag onto his shoulder. '*Parakalo, akolootha meh.*'

Jane glanced round at Ariadne, who was now standing
beside the car, and the girl arched an aristocratic brow. 'He's
waiting to show you to your room,' she said, and Jane nodded
rather irritably.

'I do understand a little Greek,' she said. Then, curbing her
frustration, 'Thank you for meeting me, Ariadne. I expect I'll
see you later.'

Ariadne's lips tightened. '*Sigoora, thespinis,*' she responded
shortly. Certainly. 'Kiria Souvakis has invited me to stay for a
few days. She thought it might be—easier—that way.'

Easier for whom? wondered Jane ruefully as she followed the
man across the paved courtyard and up shallow steps to a dappled
terrace. Scarlet fuchsias and blue and white lobelia spilled from
stone planters set at intervals along the shaded terrace, the
roofline concealed by a tumbling mass of flowering vines.

Doors stood wide to a marble-floored entrance hall which
in turn opened into a magnificent reception area. The airy feel
of the place was accentuated by huge ceiling fans that wafted
cool air into all the adjoining apartments, the concept of closing
doors not much in evidence here.

The man indicated that Jane should follow him across the
shining tiles, past a shimmering fountain whose rim was
adorned with frolicking sculptures of the gods that had once
ruled these islands. A wide open-tread staircase wound to the
upper floor and as she climbed Jane admired the many delicate
bowls of lilies that occupied every vacant surface, their vivid
colours more exotic than she'd ever seen at home.

Jane knew, from when she had used to live on the island, that the villa consisted of this two-storied central building with single-storied wings stretching out at either side. When she and Demetri had stayed here, they'd occupied a suite of rooms at the end of one of the ground-floor wings, but evidently she was to be accommodated elsewhere now.

Looking down on the scene below her, Jane was struck by the feeling of isolation she felt. Only the household staff were about, and, although she'd been hoping to escape to her room without seeing Demetri's mother, now she felt oddly insulted that none of the family was there to welcome her.

But that was probably Maria's intention, she reflected, refusing to let the other woman's attitude affect her own. Perhaps it was an attempt to show her how out-of-place she had always been here among people to whom luxury was a way of life.

Even so, the stunning beauty of high-ceilinged rooms opening one from another, of silk-clad walls and sumptuous leathers, of the staff going about on silent feet, was impressive. The Souvakis family was fabulously wealthy, after all. Which had made her relationship with Demetri so unlikely and ultimately so destructive.

A galleried landing gave access to her apartments. The room the manservant gestured for her to enter was both luxurious and comfortable. An elegant sitting room opened into a large bedroom, with glass doors giving access to a balcony from both apartments.

While the man carried her haversack inside, Jane moved across to the windows. One of the long windows was slightly ajar and she could hear the faint murmur of the sea. Below, the glassy waters of the swimming pool gleamed in the afternoon sun. But beyond the gardens, tumbling dunes gave way to a white sand shoreline, the blue-green waters of the Aegean sparkling with dazzling light.

'*Soo aresi afto, thespinis?*'

The man was asking if she liked the room and Jane turned to smile at him.

'Very much,' she said, in his own language. 'Thank you.'

'*Efkharistisi mou.*' My pleasure. He smiled warmly, and then wished her a pleasant stay before letting himself out of the room.

Jane followed him to the outer door and, when it was closed behind him, she rested back against it. She felt so tired suddenly, but she knew it was a psychological weariness as much as a physical one. She ran an exploring hand across her stomach again. Dear God, it was going to be harder than she'd imagined. She hadn't been looking forward to dealing with Demetri's mother, but she'd never dreamt she might have to contend with his future fiancée as well.

She knew she ought to unpack her few belongings, but it was too much trouble right now. Leaving the door, she kicked off her boots and, walking into the bedroom, dropped down on the bed. It was a huge bed, at least six feet across and half that again in length. But it was soft and springy and very comfortable and, flopping back against the silk coverlet, she closed her eyes.

CHAPTER SIX

THE sound of someone tapping at the door awakened her.

Jane opened her eyes and for a few moments she hadn't the first idea where she was. But then the sight of billowing sheers at the windows reminded her of her arrival. The windows had been slightly ajar, she remembered, and the sultry murmur of the sea was in her ears.

She sat up abruptly, and then grabbed the edge of the mattress as the room spun around her. Nausea gripped her, but happily it was short-lived. She'd just got up too quickly, that was all, she assured herself. She'd obviously been deeply asleep.

'*Thespinis*! *Boro na bo?*'

Whoever it was was calling her now, and Jane slid reluctantly off the bed and went to the door. She hoped it wasn't Maria. She didn't feel up to coping with her mother-in-law in crumpled trousers and a damp T-shirt. She must have been sweating while she slept and now she felt hot and sticky and totally unprepared for company.

To her relief, when she opened the door, she found one of the maids waiting outside. She was carrying a tray containing a jug of iced fruit juice and a glass, and Jane realised she was very thirsty indeed.

'Thank you,' she said, taking the tray, but, although she expected the girl to go, she evidently had something more to add.

'Kirieh Souvakis asks if you will join the family for an aperitif before supper, *thespinis?*' she requested in her own language. 'Would seven-thirty be all right?'

Jane, who had already placed the tray on the nearby table and was presently pouring herself a glass of the chilled juice, turned to blink rapidly. Then, after taking a gulp of the delicious liquid, she glanced at her watch. It was almost seven o'clock and she stared at the watch disbelievingly. She must have slept for over two hours. How rude they must think her. She hadn't even bothered to pay her respects to Demetri's father.

'Um—yes. That's fine,' she said, and then, realising the girl couldn't understand her, she amended it to, '*Neh. Ineh mia khara. Efkharisto.*'

'I will tell Kirieh Souvakis, *thespinis,*' she said, once more speaking in her own language, and Jane gave her a grateful smile before closing the door.

But once the door was closed, Jane didn't waste any more time savouring the fruit juice. Carrying the glass into the bathroom with her—which wasn't a recommended option, but she was still thirsty—she turned on the shower. Then, despite the urge to explore all the many bottles and jars that occupied the glass shelf above the basin, she stripped off her shirt, trousers and underwear and stepped beneath the cooling spray.

Half an hour later, she viewed her appearance in the long mirrors of the *armoire*. The emerald-green slip dress had thankfully taken little harm from being packed in the haversack and her high-heeled strappy sandals were a gift she'd brought herself back from her trip to Thailand.

Her legs were bare, as, too, was her complexion. Her skin was still lightly tinged with colour from her previous trip to the sun. Just mascara and eyeliner and a smear of amber lipstick was necessary, she decided. It wasn't as if anyone was going to care what she looked like. Except, perhaps, Demetri's father.

Her hair was still damp, but, combed and looped behind her ears, it didn't look out of place. The dampness gave it an unexpected streak of darker colour.

Well, she was ready, she thought, deciding against carrying a bag. Opening the outer door, she stepped out onto the landing, taking a determined gulp of air before walking towards the stairs.

It was nearly dark and the area below was lit with dozens of bulbs in ceiling sconces. Shining uplighters, standing in alcoves, shadowed delicate sculptures in gold. Even the fountain fell into a floodlit basin, bathing the hall in a magical light. Still, this was what you could do when money was no object, she mused, admiring it all with her connoisseur's eye, but not with any feeling of envy.

A maid was standing at the foot of the stairs, waiting to escort her to her hosts. She was young and her eyes moved surreptitiously over Jane's appearance, making her wonder, not for the first time, whether it was possible for anyone to suspect her secret. But no. The girl was just curious. And who could blame her?

They left the hall and followed an arching passage that led to the back of the villa. The passage was open on one side and Jane could again hear the gentle soughing of the sea. It made her wonder if Leo Souvakis was entertaining his guests outside. But before they reached the terrace the maid turned aside into an enormous glass pavilion.

The orangery, for that was what Jane remembered it was, was a veritable jungle of tropical plants and trees, with fairy lights threaded among the greenery. It was cooled during the day by a very efficient air-conditioning system, but at night only a couple of fans kept the velvety warmth at bay.

The maid announced her and then Leo Souvakis was coming towards her, leaning heavily on a cane, but with a real smile of welcome on his face. Jane registered the lines of strain on his ageing features, features which were still so remarkably like his son's. 'Jane,' he said warmly, grasping both her hands with his free one and leaning towards her to bestow a kiss on both cheeks. 'How good it is to see you. But—' He surveyed her thoroughly 'you seem positively glowing. I thought Ariadne said you looked tired when you arrived.'

'I did.' Jane returned his welcome, stifling any resentment at the thought that Ariadne had been talking about her. She allowed Demetri's father to draw her forward to meet the other people in the room. 'I'm sorry. I'm afraid I fell asleep or I'd have come to thank you for your invitation sooner. It's good to see you again, too, Leo. I won't ask how you are right now. I'm sure you must get tired of answering that question.'

'How right you are, my dear.' Leo patted her hand again and released her. 'And there's no need to apologise. Evidently that sleep has effected a cure. Now, I think you know everyone, don't you? Maria, of course.' He waited while Jane exchanged a chilly kiss with her mother-in-law and then went on, 'Ariadne, whom you met earlier. And Stefan. I'm sure you remember him. And Yanis—or should I say Father Josef?' His lips tightened unexpectedly. 'He has come especially to see you.'

Jane greeted them all in turn, grateful that, apart from Ariadne, she did indeed know everyone. Until five years ago, she had considered these people her family as well as Demetri's. Even his mother, despite the fact that she had never made her welcome.

For the next few minutes, she was busy telling them all about what she'd been doing recently. Apparently Demetri had told them about the success of the gallery, how with her help it had gone from strength to strength.

She tried not to feel warmed that he'd been impressed with the responsibilities Olga had given her, and wondered if he was trying to salve his conscience. But then, he hadn't known his father was going to invite her here when he'd returned to the island, had he?

Conversation became general and during the meal, which was taken in the adjoining dining room, Jane found herself speaking to each of them in turn. The gleaming table was wide, its orchid-entwined centrepiece lit only by flickering candles in silver sconces, and the subdued light made expressions harder to read.

Demetri's mother was still chilly and Ariadne was obviously resentful to have her here, taking centre stage in what she evidently already regarded as her domain. But Leo and his two younger sons made an effort to put her at her ease. Stefan had always been sympathetic and his malicious good humour was infectious.

The biggest change was in Yanis. When Jane left the island, he'd just been beginning his training to become a priest. Now, in black robes, and with a heavy moustache and beard, he seemed a stranger. Less approachable in some ways, though he was still as gentle as he had always been.

Jane ate little and drank less. She'd accepted a very weak *ouzo* before supper, but she refused all wine with the food. If they thought it was strange when once she'd enjoyed the wine produced on Souvakis land in the Pelopponese, it wasn't commented upon. Instead, her glass was kept filled with the iced water she'd requested.

Demetri's mother had just suggested that they might adjourn to the main salon for coffee when they all heard the throbbing beat of an aircraft overhead. Though it wasn't an aeroplane, Jane realised at once. The sound they could hear was a helicopter flying low as it came in to land.

Immediately, her mouth went dry and her palms dampened unpleasantly. She set down the glass she was holding, half afraid it was going to slip out of her hand. With all of the family—except Demetri—here, there seemed only one explanation. And as if she shared her suspicions, Ariadne's eyes widened with a mixture of surprise and anticipation.

'Demetri?' she asked, looking towards Leo Souvakis, her tongue lingering sensually at the corner of her mouth. 'But I understood he wasn't expected home until the end of the week.'

'He can't wait to see you, Ari,' declared Maria Souvakis warmly. 'Why don't you go to meet him? I'm sure Leo will excuse you.'

Before Ariadne could get out of her chair, however, Demetri's father intervened. 'It could be Vasilis, Maria. Theo Vasilis,' he added, for Jane's benefit. 'Demetri's assistant. I asked him to send me some figures earlier in the day. Perhaps he has decided to deliver them himself.'

'I think not.'

As Maria attempted to assure her husband that Demetri's assistant would never use one of the company's helicopters for his own use, Jane swallowed convulsively. Dear God, Demetri couldn't be here, could he? He'd promised...

But what had he promised? she asked herself. Only that he'd keep out of her way. He'd said nothing about staying away from the island. It was his home, after all, and Ariadne was here.

'Hardly his own use, my dear,' Leo was saying now, reaching for his cane and getting up from his seat at the head of the table. He tilted his head and Jane realised the noise had ceased. 'It seems he has landed. I will go and wait for him on the terrace.'

'I can go—' began Ariadne, but Demetri's father merely waved her offer away.

'You go into the salon with the others, my dear,' he said

charmingly. 'Enjoy your coffee. If it is Demetri, I would prefer a few moments with him alone.' He paused. 'Company matters, *katalavenis?* You understand?'

Looking from Ariadne to her mother-in-law, Jane couldn't tell which of them was the most put out by his words. 'You're supposed to take things easy!' exclaimed Maria sharply, but Leo only raised a finger to his lips.

'And I will,' he promised, making for the door. 'After I have spoken with my son.'

'And why can't Demetri speak to you in your study?' demanded Maria, going after him. 'Just because *she* is here does not mean that Demetri cannot enter his own home.'

'Jane. Her name is Jane,' said Leo tersely, his dark eyes, so like his eldest son's, flashing his displeasure. 'See to the coffee, *vineka*. I will not be long.'

He left the room without another word and for a moment there was silence in the room. Then, seizing her chance, Jane pushed back her chair and got to her feet. 'If you'll excuse me, Maria, I'd like to go to my room now. It's been a long day and I still have unpacking to attend to.'

Yeah, right. One haversack containing a couple of dresses, some shorts and tank-tops and underwear would take all of five minutes to unpack. But Demetri's mother wasn't to know that, even if Ariadne knew what she'd brought with her from the ferry.

'*Kala*—well, if you are sure?'

Jane was sure Maria—and Ariadne for that matter—couldn't believe their luck. 'I'm sure,' she said, managing a smile for Demetri's brothers. 'It's been nice to see you again, Stefan; Yanis.' *Nice!* She cringed at the word. 'If I don't see you again, thank you for making me feel so welcome.'

Leo had just reached the outer door when she entered the hall. Taking off her sandals so as not to attract his attention, she hurried across to the stairs and climbed swiftly to the upper floor. She was breathing rather unevenly, as much from nerves as exertion, when she reached the landing, and she paused for a moment to look down into the hall.

But when she heard the unmistakable sound of men's voices, she panicked. Hurrying across the landing, she hastily let herself into her room. The last thing she wanted was for Demetri to think she was eager to see him again. If she did decide to tell him about the baby, he mustn't think she expected him to change his mind about the divorce. Nothing had changed. He was still a lying bastard. After the way he'd behaved in London, she owed him nothing.

Moving across to the windows, drawn by a faint illumination, she saw the underwater lights gleaming in the pool below. She and Demetri used to swim there after dark when the rest of the household was sleeping, she remembered unwillingly. How horrified Maria would have been if she'd seen her precious son and his wife playing there in the nude.

Making love…

The images wouldn't go away, and leaving the window, she walked into the bedroom. She found someone had closed the window and switched on lamps at either side of the huge bed. The bed had been turned down, too, Egyptian sheets very white in the lamplight. And someone had also unpacked her haversack, hanging her other dress in the *armoire* and folding everything else into the drawers of the chest nearby.

Of course, Maria would have known this, Jane reflected, but her mother-in-law had made no attempt to dissuade her from leaving. And why should she? Maria hadn't wanted her here. Ariadne was the favourite in residence. Jane was just an annoying encumbrance that her husband had insisted on bringing back into their lives.

Jane tipped the straps of her dress off her shoulders and allowed it to fall about her ankles. She wasn't wearing a bra and her breasts seemed heavier than before. Stepping over the dress, she walked into the bathroom and stared at her reflection. Yes, there were definitely changes. She could see them. When she weighed her breasts in her hands, they felt different somehow.

Turning sideways, she laid both hands over her stomach. The lacy thong, which was all she was wearing now, exposed the slight swell she'd noticed before. Or perhaps she was only imagining it. She was barely six weeks, after all. How soon was a pregnancy visible? She should have asked her sister.

Or perhaps not. Lucy wouldn't have been able to resist telling their mother. And Mrs Lang would have been offended, and all hell would have broken loose. She sighed. No, it was probably best if she kept the news to herself, at least for the moment. Until she'd decided definitely what she was going to do.

'Admiring yourself, Jane?'

The voice was painfully familiar. What wasn't so familiar was the thickening emotion in his words. If she hadn't known better, she'd have said that Demetri had been aroused by watching her touch her body. How long had he been standing in the bathroom doorway? Had he seen her examining her breasts, perhaps? He must have done, she decided, her pulse quickening. That was why he was looking at her with such raw passion in his eyes.

CHAPTER SEVEN

SHE MADE herself turn her head and look away from him and for a long moment the silence stretched between them. She knew she ought to grab a towel to cover herself, but something—some perverse desire to taunt him, maybe—kept her from doing so. She wondered what he expected her to say to him. He must know his coming here like this, uninvited and unannounced, was breaking every rule in the book. They were getting a divorce, for heaven's sake. His fiancée-to-be was waiting for him downstairs. There was no way he could justify his actions. And she was a fool for not ordering him out of her suite immediately.

But all she said was, '*Déjà vu,* Demetri?' And knew he'd know exactly what she meant.

Glancing over her shoulder, she saw his hard face darken with frustration. 'Hardly,' he retorted, after a taut moment. 'Put some clothes on. I want to talk to you. I'll wait in the room next door.'

'The bedroom?'

'No, the sitting room,' he amended tersely. '*Viasoo!*' Hurry up!

Jane looked back at her reflection. 'Perhaps I don't want to put my clothes on,' she said softly. 'I came upstairs to go to bed. I'm tired. I think you should go now. I'll talk to you in the morning.'

'I won't be here in the morning,' replied Demetri through

clenched teeth. 'I have to attend a conference in Athens. It's due to last two days. I hope to be back by the end of the week.'

'And this concerns me—how?' Jane didn't know how she did it, but she put a note of sarcasm into her voice.

'Just get dressed,' he said shortly, unhooking a velvet-soft bathrobe from behind the bathroom door. He tossed it towards her. 'This will do.'

Jane made no attempt to catch the robe and it fell, unheeded, to the floor. Demetri swore in his own language and then he came towards her, his reflection joining hers in the mirror, picking up the robe and thrusting it onto her shoulders. 'Wear it.' he said roughly. 'Or I won't be responsible for my actions.'

'Ooh, I'm scared!'

Jane was beginning to enjoy this, although she realised she was playing with fire. Demetri was not a man to take her provocations lightly, and his expression made her breath catch in her throat.

'Jane,' he said, the hint of a threat in his voice, but, when he would have wrapped the folds of the robe about her, she deliberately moved away. The robe fell away once more, and Demetri's hands brushed against her breasts.

The feeling was excruciating, a mixture of throbbing sensitivity and burning desire. She wanted him to touch them, to rub the palms of his hands over their tender flesh, to bend his head and take one aching nipple into his mouth.

His eyes met hers in the mirror and she sensed he knew exactly what she was thinking. Which was a complete turn-off. She didn't want him to think she'd come here in the hope of rekindling their relationship, and, turning away, she bent and snatched up the robe, sliding her arms swiftly into the sleeves and drawing it tight across her trembling form.

'OK,' she said tersely. 'Let's go into the sitting room. I can't imagine what we have to say to one another but I'm sure you're going to tell me.'

Demetri stepped aside to allow her to precede him out of the bathroom and she was forced to brush past his still, forbidding frame. He was wearing a dark grey suit which he must have worn to whatever meeting he'd been attending that day, raw silk trousers and jacket, pearl-grey shirt, his tie pulled away from his collar. He looked disturbingly different from when he'd come to her apartment in London, but Jane knew he could look equally intimidating in turtleneck and jeans.

The living area seemed dark and Jane hastily switched on more lamps, anything to banish the sense of vulnerability she was feeling. Why had Demetri come to her rooms? Couldn't whatever he had to say wait until tomorrow morning? And then she remembered. He'd said he was leaving for Athens in the morning, so at least she would be spared the possible humiliation of him walking into the bathroom to find her throwing up.

Nevertheless, he still disturbed her. Tall, dark and dangerous, she thought, a subtle play on the familiar words. The room was suddenly smaller, closer, more intimate. And she had to get the idea that he'd somehow found out about the baby out of her head.

She wanted to sit down, but Demetri was making no attempt to do so and she was damned if she'd give him the satisfaction of inviting him to make himself at home. So, she held up her head and regarded him as coolly as she was able, while her stomach quivered and threatened to embarrass her all over again.

Demetri paused just beyond the archway that led from the bedroom. He was tired and he knew this wasn't the most sensible time to have a conversation with his soon-to-be-ex-wife. The very fact that she'd scuttled away as soon as she'd heard the helicopter proved that she'd had no wish to see him. Why hadn't he heeded his mother's words and waited until the following day before phoning her from Athens to assure himself that she'd received the divorce papers? Because the truth was he'd wanted to find out what Olga Ivanovitch had meant by calling him.

'I had a phone call,' he said now, and he could tell by the sudden tightening of her features that she was apprehensive of what was coming next.

'A call?' she echoed, her voice faintly squeaky. And then, gathering herself, 'How does this concern me?'

'The call was from Olga Ivanovitch,' said Demetri flatly, and saw the look of consternation come into her eyes. What was she afraid of?

'Olga?' She spoke lightly. 'But how—?'

'*Neh,* you are wondering how she was able to reach me?' And when she didn't say anything, he went on, 'I phoned her, you may remember? I was looking for you, to tell you my father had requested to see you, and evidently her phone recorded my number. Whatever, she made a point of taking note of it for possible future use.'

Jane swallowed. 'But why would Olga want to get in touch with you?'

Demetri shrugged. 'She did once sell my father a bronze statuette, did she not?'

The statuette that she had found, Jane remembered. Her introduction to Leonides Souvakis and ultimately his son...

Her hand moved almost protectively to the neckline of the robe. 'And was that what she wanted? To tell your father of some new item of interest she'd found?' It was unlikely, but the alternative was even less acceptable.

Demetri's mouth compressed. 'You think that is likely, bearing in mind she assumedly knows about his illness?'

Jane shivered, in spite of the heat of the room. 'I don't know what to think, do I?' she exclaimed, deciding that after all she had nothing to lose by speaking out. 'Why don't you tell me what she said instead of playing your little games of cat-and-mouse?'

'It is no game, *glika mou*.' Demetri unfastened another button at the neck of his shirt, allowing a tantalising glimpse of brown flesh lightly covered with dark hair. His eyes narrowed, thick lashes veiling his expression. 'Your employer is concerned about your health, Jane, not my father's. She told me you are *zerbrechlich*—which I believe means fragile—at the moment, *neh*? She said I should not do anything to upset you. Now, what do you think she meant by that? What have you been telling her?'

'Well, not the truth, obviously,' retorted Jane quickly, inwardly cursing Olga for making a difficult situation worse. 'You—you knew I wasn't well when you phoned me. Olga worries about me, that's all.'

'*Simfono*. With that, I agree.' He paused, and she knew he was registering the colour that had entered her pale cheeks as she spoke. 'But you told me it was just a cold. Colds do not usually elicit such concern.'

'No, well, Olga is a very—sympathetic person.' Jane made a helpless gesture. 'And—perhaps she doesn't trust you not to—not to—'

'Not to what, Jane?' The steps he took forward narrowed the space between them and she had to steel herself not to move away.

'To—to make a fool of me,' she said hurriedly, not prepared to admit that he could still hurt her. She shifted her weight from one foot to the other. And then, trying to make her tone light, 'Won't Ariadne be wondering where you are?'

'Ariadne trusts me,' he declared harshly, stung by the way she could put him on the defensive. 'What? You think I didn't tell her where I was going? That I had—how do you say—

sneaked up here to see the woman I can't wait to be free of without letting Ariadne know of my intentions?'

Jane pursed her lips. 'No.' She was defensive now.

'Good. Because you couldn't be more wrong.' Demetri didn't know where this anger had come from, but he was suddenly furious. Jane was here, in his parents' house, looking more beautiful than he'd ever seen her, and he resented it. He didn't want her here, he told himself. He didn't want to be reminded of what they'd once had. 'Ariadne and I understand one another.'

'Well, goody for you.' Now Jane felt a stirring of indignation, which was infinitely better than the embarrassment she'd felt before. 'So, if that's all you came to tell me, what are you waiting for? I'd really like to get to bed.'

Demetri's nostrils flared. And, just when he was sure he had himself under control, he asked the unforgivable, 'Why did you come here, Jane?'

Her eyes widened then. She was shocked. He could see it. And why not? It was a stupid question.

'Why did I come here?' she echoed, shaking her head. 'You know why I came, Demetri. Your father asked me to!'

'You could have refused.'

'Refused a dying man!' Jane was astounded. 'What do you think I am?'

'I don't know, do I?' Demetri's teeth ground together. 'What are you, Jane? Saint or sinner? I can't quite make up my mind.'

Her lips parted, and then, a note of contempt entering her voice, 'Well, at least I don't have that dilemma, Demetri. You're totally selfish through and through.'

'And you're not?' Demetri's lips curled, not sure why he felt this pressing need to pursue this, but unable to let it go. 'I suppose this means you've justified your reasons for walking out on me? Or do you have to keep reminding yourself why you made such a colossal mistake?'

'It wasn't a mistake!'

'*Okhi?* Why do I find that hard to believe? Isn't there something hypocritical about holding the moral high ground, when a few weeks ago you were flat on your back, letting me screw your brains out?'

The words sounded so much worse, laced as they were with his accent, and Jane gasped. Before she could prevent herself, her hand connected with his cheek.

Demetri made no attempt to deflect the blow and she watched, with a feeling of disbelief, as the clear marks of her fingers appeared on the left side of his face.

She regretted it instantly. She didn't do things like this. But it was too late to have second thoughts. Her hand had barely moved in a gesture of subjugation when Demetri's uncertain control snapped. With a savage exclamation in his own language she didn't understand, he locked hard fingers about her wrist and dragged her relentlessly towards him. 'If that's the way you want to play it, who am I to complain?'

'Demetri,' she cried, but it was no use.

'*Skaseh,*' he said harshly. Shut up!

'But you can't—'

'*Ipa skaseh,*' he repeated, grasping a handful of her hair and tipping her head backward. And then his hot mouth fastened itself to hers and she knew she was lost.

Anger, and the frustration he was feeling, made it impossible for him to be gentle with her. As he backed her up against the wall behind her, his tongue forced its way between her teeth. He pushed into her mouth, tasting her blood when his savage possession ground her lips against her teeth, but he had no mercy. He wanted to tear the bathrobe from her and bury himself inside her, and her fragile vulnerability was no deterrent, he found.

The moan she gave should have shamed him, but it didn't. The sounds she was making only served to drive him completely over the edge. Tearing the sides of the robe apart, he feasted his eyes on dusky-tipped nipples, already swollen and painfully erect, and on the slight swell of her stomach and the tight curls that hid her sex.

'*Isteh oreos,*' he muttered thickly. 'You are beautiful! *Keh ti thelo!*' And I want you!

Jane's hands had been trapped between them but now she dragged them free to rake frantic fingers across his cheek. Thankfully, she didn't draw blood, but when her nails scraped across his scalp he uttered a groan of protest.

'Do not pretend you do not want me, too,' he said unsteadily, and, although her hands had fastened in his hair with the intention of jerking his head away from hers, the shaken timbre of his voice tore her resolution to shreds.

'I—I don't,' she got out fiercely, but her lips told a different story when he kissed her again. Passion built between them with every sensual thrust of his tongue, and when he sucked her lower lip between his teeth, she could only clutch his neck and hang on.

'This is why you really came here, isn't it?' he demanded, his hands sliding possessively up her arms to tip the robe off her shoulders. 'You are determined to destroy me.'

'No,' she protested, as the robe fell to the floor, but Demetri wasn't listening to her. His fingers slid over her shoulders and down her back, caressing her hipbones briefly, before moving on to her bottom. Filling his hands with the rounded globes, he brought her deliberately against him, rotating his hips so she was made unmistakably aware of the pressure of his erection.

'Do you feel that?' he asked, his voice thick with emotion. 'Yes, of course you do. But do you have any idea what it's like to be this close to you and not be a part of you?'

'Demetri—'

'You drive me crazy,' he went on, as if she hadn't spoken, thrusting his thigh between her legs. 'Stark, staring crazy, and I still want you even closer to me, under me, spreading your legs for me, to give me some relief from this torment you're putting me through.'

'Demetri—'

'Do not try to tell me I don't know what I'm saying,' he snarled. 'I know. I know, Jane. Believe me.'

'Demetri, please—'

The husky tone of her voice vibrated through him, but he was too far gone to listen to reason. Tucking a hand beneath the tumbled silk of her hair, he tipped her head up to his, his mouth silencing any further protest.

The kiss was deep and erotic, an affirmation of everything he'd been saying, seducing her to a place where nothing mattered but that he should go on kissing her and caressing her, drenching her body in the mindless heat of her own arousal.

She wondered afterwards if he would have taken her there, against the wall of her sitting room, if they hadn't been interrupted. Demetri was already using his free hand to tear his shirt open, dragging off his tie to send it spiralling across the room. And she—God help her!—was encouraging him, cupping his warm neck between her palms, digging her nails into taut flesh that smelled hot and sweaty and deliciously male.

She was rubbing herself against him, delighting in the sensual brush of his body hair against her breasts, when there was a tentative knock on the door.

For a moment, neither of them moved. It was as if they

were suddenly frozen, blood cooling to weld them to the spot. Demetri, his face buried in the scented curve of her shoulder, breathed a word that could more politely be described as 'Damn!' and slumped against her. And Jane tipped her head back against heavy silk damask, grateful for the wall's support.

'Jane!'

Her mouth went dry. The momentary fear that it was Demetri who'd spoken, alerting whoever was on the other side of the door to his presence, making her feel weak. But almost immediately she realised that Demetri was too enraged to say anything civil. It was another voice that was disconcertingly like Demetri's who had spoken her name.

With a strength she hadn't known she possessed, Jane managed to push Demetri's head back so he could see her lips. 'It's your father,' she mouthed, the consternation evident in her face, and with a resigned gesture he muttered, 'I know.'

'So what are you going to do about it?' she continued as he dragged himself upright and raked back his hair. She bent to snatch the bathrobe from the floor and quickly put it on. 'He can't find you here. Not like this. You've got to go.'

'Go where?' He was sardonic. 'Do you expect me to hide in the bathroom until he's gone?'

'That's one idea, certainly.' Jane swallowed and nodded her head, but Demetri only gave her a scornful look.

'*Apoklieteh!*' he whispered harshly. 'No way!'

'Jane!' There was a pregnant pause and then Leo Souvakis spoke again. 'Is someone with you, *kiria?* I can come back later, if you would rather?'

'No, I—'

Jane struggled for an answer, gazing beseechingly at Demetri, begging him to get out of sight.

But all he did was finish fastening the buttons on his shirt and stuff it back into his trousers. Then, to her horror, he walked across to the door and swung it open.

CHAPTER EIGHT

To HER surprise, Jane slept amazingly well.

She hadn't expected to. After the day—and evening—she'd had, she'd anticipated lying awake for hours, mulling over everything that had happened. But instead, she'd lost consciousness the moment her head hit the pillow.

A clear conscience? She didn't think so. What she'd done—what she'd allowed Demetri to do—had been unforgivable. She'd deserved to spend the night berating herself for her foolishness.

No doubt the fact that she was pregnant had had something to do with the ease with which she'd fallen asleep, she reflected ruefully. Now, rolling onto her back, she found the sun streaming through the crack in the curtains she'd drawn the night before. While she'd been in London, fretting over the alternatives she was faced with, such sleep as she'd had had been restless and plagued with tortuous dreams. But last night she'd been so exhausted, she hadn't been able to keep her eyes open.

In consequence she felt rested, more rested than she'd done in a long time. Not since Demetri had come back into her life, in fact.

However, it was time to get up and face the day and it wasn't just the familiar nausea that was causing her stomach to quiver in protest. Dear God, what had Demetri's father really thought when his son had thrown open her door and stormed out of her apartments without a word of explanation the night before? Just a terse 'Papa' in passing, and then he strode away towards the stairs as if he at least had no intention of answering any questions about his reasons for being there.

What Leo Souvakis must have thought, finding his son with the woman he was supposed to be divorcing was anyone's guess. And not 'supposed to be divorcing', Jane amended. *Was* divorcing. Hadn't she received the initial papers the day before she'd left for Kalithi? Just because she hadn't signed them yet didn't make them any the less real.

Pushing back the covers, she discovered she'd slept without the man-size T-shirt she invariably wore. But being left to face Leo's obvious confusion when his son had passed him with barely an acknowledgement had been humiliating, so it was no wonder she'd been bewildered after he'd gone. At the time, however, Demetri's father had gazed after his son as if he didn't understand the situation. And then he'd looked at Jane and found she was wearing only a bathrobe and an expression of understanding had crossed his lined face.

Jane's own face had been burning. She'd been all too aware that her lips were bruised and she had stubble burns on her cheeks. Leo wasn't a fool. He must have guessed exactly what he'd interrupted. Which was why he'd refused when she'd invited him in.

'Ah, not tonight, Jane,' he'd said, glancing once again along the landing, almost as if he'd expected his son to reappear. 'If you have everything you need, I'll wish you goodnight. Sleep well, my dear. *Kalinikhta.*'

He'd obviously decided now was not the time to indulge in casual conversation. But as Jane had said goodnight, she'd wished she'd had the nerve to say *It's not what you think!* Yet it *was* what he'd probably thought, she admitted unhappily.

How could she pretend otherwise? And what he'd thought of her behaviour, let alone his son's, was not something she was looking forward to finding out.

A maid brought her breakfast while Jane was taking her shower. She found the tray containing fruit juice, sweet rolls and coffee on her bedside table when she came out of the bathroom. She hoped the girl hadn't heard anything she shouldn't, but if she had, what of it? People were sick for various reasons, not all of them suspicious.

The smell of coffee was offputting, but, breaking off a corner of one of the rolls, she popped it into her mouth. It was good. It even made her feel a little better, and she remembered that she'd read somewhere that food could help morning sickness.

She ate two of the rolls and drank the fruit juice, her spirits improving all the time. She even swallowed half a cup of coffee and by the end she was feeling pretty good.

The maid who'd unpacked her clothes had folded all the casual items into a drawer. Jane pulled out a sleeveless tank-top, in pink with matching shorts. The colour suited her and she secured her hair with a long-toothed comb. Then, feeling a little apprehensive, she left her room. It was after nine, so perhaps someone would be about.

She wasn't thinking about Demetri, she told herself as she descended the stairs, though she couldn't help wondering if he'd left. But it was Stefan she saw first, picking out a tune on a magnificent baby grand piano in the music room, where long arched windows opened to the terrace beyond.

Crossing the hall, she paused in the entrance, and, although he couldn't have heard her silent approach, he lifted his head. 'Jane!' he exclaimed, getting up from the stool to reveal that like her he was wearing shorts and a casual shirt. He came towards her, smiling warmly. 'Did you sleep well? You were not too tired after—after your journey?'

His hesitation was telling, but Jane chose not to notice it. 'Very well,' she said, wondering if his mother would approve of the air kisses he bestowed on each of her cheeks. 'I gather you're not working today.'

When she'd left the island, Stefan had been acting as his father's secretary. But, knowing Leo as she did, Jane couldn't believe he'd approve of Stefan's attire if he was working with him.

'Not today,' he agreed, without offering any further explanation. 'Have you had breakfast? I can ask Angelena—'

'I've eaten, thanks.' Jane glanced about the sunlit salon. 'This is a lovely room. And so quiet. I'd forgotten how quiet Kalithi could be.'

'How dull, you mean,' said Stefan drily, and Jane wondered if she'd only imagined the bitterness in his voice. The night before, he'd seemed reasonably happy. But now there was a distinct air of melancholy about his plump features.

'I suppose that depends what you're looking for,' she murmured, not really wanting to get into any in-depth discussion about his life.

'So what are you looking for, Jane?' Stefan's brows arched and his tone was faintly malicious. 'Is being a success in business really all you want from life?'

'I don't know what I want,' said Jane bluntly, and it was nothing but the truth. 'Um—where is everyone? Having breakfast?'

'My father rarely comes down before lunch,' replied Stefan carelessly. 'My mother usually spends the morning with him, though, with Ariadne being here, she may decide to change her routine. Yanis has returned to the seminary, and—my other brother left over an hour ago.'

'Demetri?' Jane was amazed. She hadn't even heard the helicopter. But also relieved, she told herself. It had to be easier now he was gone.

'Demetri,' Stefan agreed. 'He expects to be back tomorrow evening.'

'Tomorrow evening!'

'Yes, tomorrow evening.' Stefan regarded her with some amusement. 'So, how do you propose to entertain yourself until then?'

Jane's colour deepened. 'I don't know what you mean. I didn't come here to see Demetri.'

'No?' He didn't sound convinced and she wondered if that was what his father and mother thought, too. Not to mention Demetri himself. But she didn't want to think about him.

'Your father asked to see me,' she said now. She linked her hands together. 'I couldn't—I didn't *want* to refuse.'

'Humph.' Stefan shrugged his shoulders. He was of a shorter build than Demetri and there was something essentially feminine about his mocking smile. 'If you say so, who am I to disagree with you? Perhaps I'm allowing Mama's influence to colour my judgement.'

Jane shook her head and would have retreated into the hall in search of friendlier company, when he spread his arms disarmingly. 'I'm sorry,' he said. 'I'm a bitch, I know. You mustn't take any notice of me, Jane. Come: let me take you for a walk. We can go down through the garden and onto the beach.'

Jane hesitated. 'Oh, I don't know whether—'

'Please.' Stefan could be charming when he chose. 'Or we could sit by the pool. I know how you like to swim.'

She might have taken that as another sly comment but at present putting on a swimsuit might be unwise. In consequence, she decided to accept Stefan's former offer. 'A walk sounds— appealing,' she said, crossing her arms and cupping her elbows in her palms. It had to be better than hanging about here waiting for her mother-in-law or Ariadne to appear.

They left the house through sliding doors that opened from the morning room. This part of the villa looked much the same as Jane remembered, with duck-egg-blue walls, yellow and white pottery on glass-topped tables and a cool marble floor. Half-drawn Roman blinds in shades of green and brown and orange should have clashed with the vivid décor, but they didn't. It was a cheerful room, spoilt only by the memory of the argument she and Demetri had had here the morning before she left the island for good.

Or what she'd thought was for good, she reflected, preceding Stefan through the sliding doors. Now there was so much confusion inside her, she didn't know what she thought.

Thankfully the terrace held no such horrors. Italian tiles, vine-hung trellises, marble steps leading down to a huge circular pool. They bypassed the steps and the cedar-wood cabins that housed both showers and a sauna, following a path that led between lawns that were presently being watered by an efficient sprinkler system. The lawns were edged with bushes of flowering cactus, the path paved and immaculately free of any weeds.

It was all very lush, very beautiful, but also incredibly hot. Jane, who hadn't thought about buying sunscreen when she'd packed her bag, hoped she wouldn't get burned. But nothing about this trip was turning out as she'd anticipated and she had to seriously revise her expectations.

There was a welcome breeze blowing when they stepped onto the sand and Jane kicked off her sandals and carried them by their straps. The sand wasn't yet hot enough to burn her feet and she walked purposefully towards the water.

'*Eh! Pio arga!* Slow down,' exclaimed Stefan, hurrying after her. 'We have all morning.'

You may have, thought Jane drily, but she didn't say it. Nevertheless, she had to wonder why Stefan was content to laze his days away here on the island when it seemed obvious his father was doing very little work at the moment.

The waves curled about her bare feet, their initial coldness giving way to a delicious warmth. This was the best time of the day to swim, she remembered ruefully. Before the sun could burn you even through the water.

'You have to learn to relax, Jane,' Stefan said, puffing a little as he came up beside her. 'You are not in England now.'

'Do you think I don't know that?' Jane kept her eyes on her feet, watching as the sand slid away beneath them. Then she shrugged and looked up at him. 'What are you doing here, Stefan? Have you been sent to keep an eye on me?'

Stefan gave her a wounded look. 'Do you think I would agree to that?'

Jane arched a mocking brow. 'I'll take that as a yes, shall I?'

'No!' He was indignant. 'I thought you might be glad of some company, is all.'

Jane regarded him intently for a few seconds and then she turned away. 'OK.' She started to walk along the sand, her feet in the shallows. 'So tell me what you've been doing. Don't you work for your father any more?'

Stefan's mouth compressed. 'I'm sure you're not interested in my problems, Jane. But I am intrigued by your relationship with Demetri. Are you aware he's going to marry Ariadne as soon as his divorce is absolute?'

'Yes, he told me.'

'And did he tell you why?'

Jane sighed. 'Is this relevant, Stefan? Demetri wants a divorce. End of story.'

'No, it's not the end of the story,' retorted Stefan shortly.

'There was no need for Demetri to get a divorce, not unless he chose to do so, of course.'

Jane frowned. 'What do you mean?'

'I mean I was perfectly willing to give our father the grand-child he so desperately craves. But I was not good enough. My relationship with Phillippe is not good enough, despite the fact that we have been together for over six years.'

Jane halted to stare at him in disbelief. 'You mean, you and Phillippe Martin are—are—'

'A couple? Yes.' Stefan raised dark brows. 'Of course, you met him, did you not? Didn't Demetri tell you we lived together?'

'He said you were—friends,' said Jane, feeling enormously stupid. Even when Demetri had told her Stefan wasn't inter-ested in women, she still hadn't put two and two together.

'Of course, I shouldn't be surprised.' Stefan was walking on now, kicking the water into a spray ahead of him. 'Demetri is our father's heir. The eldest son. The golden boy! No one else's child is good enough.'

Jane shook her head. Did Demetri know this? Had he any idea how Stefan felt? Or course, he must do. The situation was too raw not to have been discussed between Demetri and his father at some point.

'I'm sorry,' she said, knowing that was inadequate but not knowing what else to say, and Stefan gave her a reluctant smile.

'*Then pirazi,*' he said philosophically. It doesn't matter. 'Shall we go a little further?'

They walked about a quarter of a mile along the beach and then turned back. To Jane's relief, their conversation had shifted to less personal things and she was so busy trying to avoid any controversial topics that she completely forgot how hot it was.

But by the time they left the beach and threaded their way back to the terrace, she could feel her shoulders prickling. A hasty glance informed her that her arms were very red, too, and she could only guess that her face looked like a beetroot.

Which was so galling when she saw both her mother-in-law and Ariadne sitting on the terrace, securely shaded by a fringed striped canopy.

It took a great deal of courage to continue walking towards them, particularly as she was feeling a little faint now and distinctly dizzy. A situation that wasn't helped when Stefan excused himself and continued on into the villa, leaving Jane to face the two women on her own.

'Ah, Jane,' said Maria at once, her shrewd eyes quickly assessing how her daughter-in-law must be feeling. 'Why don't you come and join us? We were just having coffee.'

Jane knew Maria had no real desire for her company. It was just her way of making an embarrassing situation worse. She obviously knew that Jane would have preferred to go to her room to put some salve on her arms and shoulders, but she couldn't resist any opportunity to torment her.

And Jane, desperate not to do anything to worsen the situation, forced a tight smile, and said, 'Thank you,' before sinking weakly into the cushioned chair beside Ariadne.

But even the smell of the coffee was sickening, and, when Maria summoned the maid to get another cup, Jane licked her dry lips and said, 'Would you mind if I just had water?'

'Water?' Maria gazed at her impatiently. 'What's wrong? Aren't you well?'

'I'm hot,' said Jane quickly, desperate not to arouse suspicion. 'And very thirsty. If you don't mind?'

'She's not used to our climate,' remarked Ariadne scornfully. 'She looks like a cooked lobster, Maria. Perhaps she would prefer to go to her room.'

Jane objected to being spoken about as if she wasn't there,

but she was so grateful to the other girl for saying what she had, she didn't complain.

'I think I would prefer to do that, Maria, if you don't mind,' she murmured, getting to her feet again on legs that felt distinctly unsteady. 'Perhaps you could ask the maid to bring the water upstairs?'

Maria's mouth tightened. 'Surely you can stay for a few minutes, Jane? We haven't had an opportunity to talk together yet. Don't you want to know how my husband is feeling this morning?'

'Of course I want to know how Leo is,' protested Jane, sinking obediently back into her chair. 'I just thought—'

'I can imagine what you thought. You would prefer not to have this conversation, I have no doubt,' Maria interrupted her sharply. 'But let us be clear about something, Jane. I did not approve of Leo inviting you here. No matter what he says, you are not welcome in my home. Now that you've seen him, I hope you'll make your excuses and leave as soon as decently possible, *neh?*'

Jane expelled a shaken breath. 'Why did you allow Demetri to contact me?' she exclaimed. 'Why didn't you just pretend that you'd spoken to me and that I'd refused to come?'

'Because Leo would never have accepted that. And I care too much about Demetri to deliberately lie to him.'

Jane shook her head and then wished she hadn't. The dizziness she'd felt coming up from the beach had come back and she clutched desperately at the arms of her chair in an effort to steady herself.

Unfortunately, both Ariadne and Maria noticed and her mother-in-law gave an impatient snort. 'Oh, go to your room, then,' she said irritably. 'If you can't control yourself for five minutes, then you'd better do as Ariadne says. But don't forget what I've told you, will you? Next time I might not be half so understanding.'

Whatever that meant.

CHAPTER NINE

DEMETRI FLEW back to the island late the following afternoon. He hadn't stayed to hear the final conclusions of the delegates to the conference, making the excuse that, as his father was so ill, he'd prefer to get home.

And, without exception, everyone had understood, but he couldn't help wondering if they'd have been as understanding if they'd known that checking up on his father encompassed only half the concerns he had. He was equally anxious to see Jane again, to assure himself that she hadn't been intimidated in his absence.

He didn't know why he felt this desperate need to defend his estranged wife, but he did. It wasn't as if she'd be glad to see him. Because, despite the fact that he didn't seem able to keep his hands off her, he was fairly sure she regretted it just as much as he did.

Nevertheless, when his pilot landed the helicopter on the pad a couple of hundred yards from the villa, he breathed a sigh of relief. Without waiting for Vasilis to swing open the door and let down the steps, he accomplished the task himself and dropped down gratefully onto the tarmac.

'I won't need you tonight, Theo,' he said when the other man joined him. 'You can go home, if you wish.' Theo's parents lived on one of the other islands in the group. 'Costas will take you.'

'If it's all the same to you, I'd like to stay at the cottage,' said Theo, mentioning one of a cluster of stone dwellings where many of the staff who worked on the estate lived. He set down the two briefcases he was carrying and stowed the steps back inside the aircraft. 'I'm hoping to see Ianthe, if you have no objections?'

'Why would I object?' Demetri raised a hand to the pilot as Costas prepared to take off again. 'She's a free woman.'

'I know that, but—'

'But what?'

'Well…' Theo looked embarrassed now. 'It's common knowledge that you and she were once—were once—'

'Friends,' said Demetri harshly. 'We were friends, Theo. Friends! Not lovers, as I'm sure you've heard.'

'But your wife—'

'She didn't believe me either,' said Demetri, his pleasant mood evaporating. 'Forget it. It's all in the past now. Perhaps one day Ianthe will tell you who Marc's father really was. Until then, take my word for it, I wish you—both of you—nothing but good luck. OK?'

'Thanks.'

Demetri picked up his own briefcase and the two men separated as they reached the house, Theo to circle the villa to where the cottages were situated and Demetri to run lightly up the steps and into the reception hall.

The place seemed deserted, but almost immediately his mother appeared from the direction of the terrace. 'Demetri!' she exclaimed, evidently surprised to see him. 'Is something wrong?'

'Why should anything be wrong, Mama?' Demetri felt a sense of impatience that was out of all proportion to the perceived offence. 'I went to the conference as I promised and now I'm back.' He paused. 'Where's my father?' It was better than asking whether Jane was still here.

Maria Souvakis clicked her tongue. 'You may well ask,' she said, and it was obvious she wasn't pleased with the answer she had to give him. 'He's gone for a drive with that woman, hasn't he? I warned him that it was unwise to overtax himself, but he won't listen to me.'

Demetri knew exactly who his mother meant, and his relief was so great he didn't consider his words before saying, 'I doubt if taking a drive with Jane will overtax him greatly, Mama.'

But then a frown formed between his brows. What was he saying? He wanted Jane out of his life, didn't he? Encouraging his father to make her visit a pleasant one was hardly the action of a sensible man.

'I might have known you'd disagree with me,' declared Maria tersely. 'After all, you're the one who brought her here.'

Demetri let that go, but his mother wasn't finished. 'Thank goodness, Ariadne has gone with them,' she continued. 'She'll make sure your father doesn't do anything stupid.'

Demetri blew out a breath. 'Anything stupid?'

'Like inviting her to stay indefinitely,' she explained irritably. Then, as if realising this was hardly the way to greet her son after he'd been away, she tucked her arm through his. 'Come along. Thermia's here. We're having iced tea on the terrace. She'll be pleased to see you.'

Demetri doubted that. And the last person he wanted to see right now was Ianthe's mother. Was Ianthe with her? Could he really be that unlucky?

Remaining rooted to the spot when his mother would have drawn him across the hall, he said wearily, 'Give me a break, Ma. I'm hot and tired. What I really need is a shower and something a little stronger than iced tea!'

'Nonsense.' His mother was having none of that. 'What would Thermia think if you didn't come and say hello?'

Demetri's jaw tightened. 'Is she alone?'

'Of course not. Ianthe's with her. And I know she'll be glad of some younger company.'

Iperokha! Great! Demetri suppressed a groan. Who had invited the Adonides women here? But he didn't really need to ask. Nevertheless, Theo was going to be so disappointed when he drove into town to find Ianthe wasn't home.

Contrary to what his mother had said, Ianthe looked less than happy to see him. 'Demetri,' she murmured politely after he had greeted her mother. 'Aunt Maria said you wouldn't be back before tomorrow.' Ianthe had always called his mother 'aunt' but it was only an honorary title. The two women were actually distant cousins, even if they behaved more like sisters.

Now Demetri cast his mother a sardonic look, but she busied herself taking another glass from the chilled cabinet the maid had placed beside her. 'You'll have some iced tea, won't you, Demetri?'

'Not for me,' he said, aware that Ianthe was exchanging a furtive look with her mother. 'I can't stay. Now that I know my father's OK, I'd like to get home.'

Maria straightened, the glass in her hand. 'But Demetri, you can't mean to leave without seeing your father?'

'I'll see him later,' insisted Demetri through his teeth. 'Right now, I'd like to catch Theo before he leaves for town.'

'Theo is here?'

It was Ianthe who'd spoken, and Demetri saw a look of unguarded anticipation in her eyes.

'Yeah,' he said. 'He's staying the night in the cottage. D'you want to see him?'

'Oh, well—'

'I don't think so, Demetri.'

Ianthe and her mother spoke in unison but it was Maria

Souvakis who had the final word. 'Why would Ianthe want to see Theo Vasilis, Demetri?' she demanded. 'For heaven's sake, Thermia was just telling me that Ianthe's had more than a dozen text messages from that young man while you've been away. He's becoming a positive nuisance!'

Demetri arched a brow at Ianthe. 'Is that true?'

'That he's texted me, yes.'

'I meant the bit about him being a nuisance,' said Demetri patiently. 'He seems to think you like his company.'

Ianthe glanced awkwardly from her mother to her aunt and back again. 'Well—I do—like him,' she mumbled uncertainly and the older women exchanged an impatient look.

'So?' Demetri was getting impatient himself. 'Do you want to see him or not?' And when she kept her eyes averted, he added irritably, 'You're twenty-three, Ianthe. If you want to be friends with him, no one can stop you.'

'Demetri!'

His mother, who had seated herself beside Thermia, now looked up at him with horrified eyes, but Demetri had had enough. 'Well?' he said, pointedly, and with another anxious look in her mother's direction, Ianthe got to her feet.

'Yes, I'd like to see him,' she muttered humbly, and with a muffled oath Demetri bid a terse farewell to his mother and Thermia, and stepped back into the house with Ianthe at his heels.

They were crossing the reception hall when Demetri heard the unmistakable sound of a car coming up the drive to the house and his stomach clenched instinctively. Oh, right, he thought tiredly, wasn't this just par for the course? He'd thought things couldn't get any worse, but they just had.

'That must be your father and Ariadne and—and your wife,' offered Ianthe uneasily, and Demetri gave her a wry look.

'Yes,' he said flatly. 'I think you're right. How wonderful!'

Ianthe's eyes held an expression of reproach. 'You don't mean that.'

'Don't I?' Despite his reluctance, Demetri continued doggedly towards the outer doors. 'Well, we'll see, shall we?'

They paused in the open doorway as his father's vintage Bentley halted at the foot of the steps that led up to the terrace where they were standing. Unaware of being observed, Jane was first out of the car. She'd apparently been acting as his father's chauffeur with him beside her in the front seat. Now, she hurried round the bonnet to pull open his door, offering him a hand to alight. He did so gratefully, leaning heavily on her arm before rescuing his cane and transferring his weight to it.

'Thank you, my dear,' he said with evident warmth. And then he saw his son.

'Demetri!' he exclaimed, and Ariadne, who had been getting rather ill-temperedly out of the back of the car, lifted her head disbelievingly.

'Darling,' she cried, ignoring Jane and his father. Darting ahead of them, she reached Demetri and, grasping his free arm, she stood on tiptoe to brush her mouth against his. 'You're back!'

'You noticed.' Demetri's tone was even, but he was watching his wife and his father making their careful ascent of the steps. Then, with an inward curse, he put down his briefcase and went to help them, leaving Ariadne and Ianthe to exchange an unfriendly look.

'I can manage,' said his father irritably, and Jane permitted her husband a contemptuous stare.

'Hoping to impress your girlfriends?' she asked but the smile she'd adopted for his father's benefit turned malicious when she looked at him.

'Well, obviously I'm not impressing you,' he retorted,

ignoring his father's protests and taking his full weight on his shoulder. 'And believe it or not, I didn't know Ianthe was coming here today.'

'It's of no interest to me whether you did or not,' declared Jane, not altogether truthfully. She directed her whole attention to the old man. 'Not much further, Leo.'

'I see that.' Demetri's father shook his head. 'But I'm not an invalid, you know.'

'You're not used to climbing steps,' pointed out Demetri drily as they reached the level surface of the terrace. 'OK.' He released his father's arm. 'You're on your own now.'

'Thank you.' Leo's tone was clipped, but then, noticing Ianthe's anxious expression, his voice softened. 'Hello, little one. Where are you and Demetri off to?'

'*We're* not going anywhere,' Demetri answered him, his irritation increasing with every word his father spoke.

'I'm going to see Theo,' Ianthe explained nervously. 'Demetri says he's staying at the cottage.'

'Ah.' The old man nodded. 'And does your mother approve?'

'Whether her mother approves or not isn't relevant,' said Demetri angrily, and his father gave him a warning look.

'Just because you do exactly as you like, don't expect the same behaviour from everyone else,' he said coldly. He glanced round for Jane. 'Come, my dear, will you give me your arm?'

Jane looked uncomfortable now, and well she should, thought Demetri furiously. This was not why he'd brought her here, to drive a wedge between him and his father. Dammit, he'd had just about enough of this.

'I'd like to speak to my wife, if you can spare her for five minutes,' he said, ignoring Ariadne's disapproval. They weren't engaged yet, he told himself grimly, even if it was only a matter of time.

His father sucked in an impatient breath. 'Can't it wait, boy?' he demanded, and that word was the last straw.

'No, it can't,' said Demetri flatly. 'Jane: will you come into the library? We can talk there.'

Jane glanced about her a little desperately, but she knew she'd get no help from either Ariadne or Ianthe. Leo, after a resigned shrug of his shoulders, had already begun to make his way across the smooth marble floor, proving he didn't need her help.

'I—suppose so,' she conceded finally, with ill grace. She met Ianthe's anxious gaze. 'Don't worry. I won't keep him long.'

'Oh, for pity's sake!' Demetri gripped her arm just above her elbow and guided her decisively towards the arched corridor that led into the west wing of the villa. Then, as if feeling some remorse for the way he was treating Ariadne, he looked back and added, 'I'll see you at dinner, Ari. We'll have the whole evening to ourselves. I promise.'

Ariadne's face softened. '*Endaxi.*' OK. Her tongue circled her pink lips. '*Saghapo.*' I love you.

Demetri made no response to this, but he could tell that Jane knew exactly what Ariadne had said. Her arm stiffened and, if she could have wrenched herself free of him, she would have done so. As it was, he had to virtually frogmarch her into the book-lined apartment and slam the heavy door behind them.

Only then did he release her, and she quickly put some space between them. She went to stare out of the windows, windows that overlooked a cascade of flowering plants and shrubs falling away below them. From here, the sea looked distant, with acres of woodland marking the boundary of the Souvakis' property. But the backdrop was spectacular, the sea darkening from aqua-marine to deepest sapphire.

The silence stretched, and Jane, who had determined not to be the first to speak, found her nerves growing as taut as violin strings. As always on occasions like these, she worried that he'd somehow found out about the baby. But surely if he had, she'd have heard about it before now.

Hearing the rustle of papers, she felt compelled to turn, half expecting him to be holding a private letter from her doctor. But that was so ludicrous, she couldn't believe she'd even considered it, and she was a little put out to discover he was riffling through some papers on his father's desk.

Almost trembling with indignation, she exclaimed, 'What do you think you're doing, Demetri? You invited me in here and now you're apparently reading your father's mail. If this is some kind of power play, forget it.'

Demetri remained bent over the desk, but he looked up at her through his lashes. 'It's no power play,' he told her, his eyes dropping once again to his task. Then, almost against his will, he added, 'You seem to have my father under your spell.'

Jane gasped. 'And that's what you wanted to tell me?'

'No.' At last, Demetri straightened, tossing the letter he had been examining aside. 'I wanted to ask if you'd received the divorce papers from Carl Gerrard. They should have been with you a week ago, before you left for the island.'

Jane's nostrils flared. 'Well, they weren't,' she retorted, excusing her answer on the grounds that the papers only arrived four days ago.

Demetri's brows drew together. 'You're sure about that?'

'That they didn't arrive a week ago?' she asked innocently. 'Oh, yes, I'm very sure.'

Demetri came round the desk to prop his hips against the huge slab of granite that formed its surface and folded his arms. 'Well, that's very strange,' he said, regarding her with disturbing intent. 'When I spoke to him this morning, he assured me the papers had been sent.'

'Blame the post office,' she said, casually edging towards the door. 'And now, if you'll excuse me, I'd like to go and freshen up.'

'*Akomi*. Not yet.' He didn't move but she knew as surely as if he had that she wouldn't be leaving until he was finished with her. 'Tell me,' he continued mildly. 'When are you planning to return to England?'

Jane wrapped her arms about her midriff. 'Are you wanting rid of me?'

Demetri's lips thinned. 'I simply want to know what you've told my father.'

'And not just about when I'm leaving, I'll bet,' she said provocatively. 'Don't worry, Demetri. I haven't told anyone what happened at my apartment.'

Demetri's nostrils flared. 'You say that as if it was a threat.'

'No.' Jane backed off from a full confrontation. 'I'm just reassuring you that you have nothing to fear from me.'

'To fear?' He seemed determined to have an argument. 'Why should I fear you, Jane? I'm sure Ariadne wouldn't be interested in anything you had to say.'

'You mean, she wouldn't believe me? More fool her.'

Demetri's face darkened. 'Are you saying you regret what happened?'

Jane's jaw dropped. 'Are you joking? Of course I regret it.'

'Why?' There was an edge of scorn to his tone now. 'It's not as if it was anything new for you. According to that witch you call an employer, you and your boyfriend spend a lot of time at your apartment.'

'That's not true!' Jane couldn't let him get away with that and she wished, not for the first time, that Olga would keep her nose out of her affairs.

'Why should I believe you?'

'Because Alex hasn't even been in my apartment. Don't

judge everybody by your own standards, Demetri. Whatever you may think, I don't sleep around.'

Demetri's eyes narrowed. 'So what do you do together?'

'It's none of your business.'

'Humour me.'

'No.' Jane had had enough of this. 'I don't ask what you and Ariadne do together. I don't care so long as it doesn't concern me. I don't believe I even asked what you and Ianthe did together.' Her lips curled. 'I didn't have to. I knew.'

CHAPTER TEN

'YOU knew nothing!'

Demetri came up off the desk in one swift, menacing lunge and Jane felt the hairs on the back of her neck prickle alarmingly. He was so big, so dark, so powerful. So *angry!* She couldn't help herself. She automatically backed away from him.

And found her way blocked by the leather armchair in the window embrasure behind her. It smacked into her calves and, with a little gasp of surprise, she subsided onto the seat. Demetri loomed over her and for a moment she thought he was going to strike her. But he didn't. What he did was bend towards her, gripping the arms of the chair, effectively imprisoning her in place.

'OK,' he said harshly, his breath hot against skin that was still slightly tender from the sun. She was wearing a cropped tank-top and a cream denim skirt and her sudden descent had driven the skirt halfway up her thighs. 'Here it is for the last time, *aghapi.* I have slept with Ariadne, I don't deny it. I have never slept with Ianthe.'

Jane couldn't deny the twist of pain she felt at hearing him admit that he and Ariadne were lovers, but she managed to say bitterly, 'Someone did.'

'But not me.'

'Then why did she say it was?' Jane demanded raggedly.

'Same answer as before: you'd have to ask her,' replied Demetri tersely. 'Maybe this time she'll tell you the truth.'

Jane swallowed, permitting herself a look up into his dark face. 'What I find hard to understand is how you can even associate with her if she was lying.'

'To begin with, I couldn't. But my mother—'

'Oh, right.' Jane shook her head. 'I might have known your mother would have some part in this.'

'She is fond of Ianthe,' said Demetri through his teeth. 'She regards her as family.'

'The way she never regarded me.'

Demetri sighed. 'OK. I know it was hard for you. But it would have got easier.'

'Before or after you'd slept with Ianthe?'

'I've told you—'

'All right, all right.' Jane shrugged. 'I still don't understand why it should matter to you what I think now.'

Demetri's breath sharpened. 'Because it does.'

'Why?'

'Why do you think?'

Jane's lips twisted. 'Because no one is allowed to contradict the great Demetri Souvakis?' she suggested scornfully. 'Or do you just like tormenting me?'

'Do I do that?'

His voice had thickened and this time, when Jane chanced a glance through her lashes, she surprised an odd humility in his expression.

She shivered. 'You know you do.'

'How?'

She spread her hands, indicating his arms and her confinement. 'Need I say more?'

Demetri's eyes darkened, but he had to acknowledge that she was right. 'OK,' he said. 'Point taken.' But he didn't move. 'Perhaps you ought to ask yourself why.'

'Why you like tormenting me?'

'I didn't say I liked it,' he corrected her, and now his voice was harsh with emotion. He lifted a hand, which he noticed wasn't quite steady, and took hold of her chin, turning her face up to his. 'You still drive me crazy and you know it.'

Jane trembled. He could feel it. Goosepimples appeared on her shoulders, ran down her arms to the hands that were clenched in her lap. A wave of colour swept up from her throat and into her face, warming the flesh beneath his fingers. And Demetri—God help him, he thought grimly—couldn't stop himself from dropping down onto his haunches in front of her and covering her mouth with his.

A soft moan escaped her lips, her breath filling his lungs with the taste and the smell of her. Demetri came down on one knee then and, cupping her face in his hands, he deepened the kiss until her lips parted on a gasp and he was able to plunge his tongue into her open mouth.

The sensation was exquisite: taut muscle against soft wet flesh, and it was all too easy to remember how hot and tight she'd been when he'd pushed his sex inside her. His senses swam at the memory. A mindless kind of self-destruction was driving him on. And the throbbing pulse of his erection was like a drum beating in his head.

'Demetri,' she protested, but it was barely audible. Did she really expect him to stop? When he released her mouth to seek the scented hollow of her throat her breathing quickened. And she didn't try to pull away.

His mouth and teeth were seducing her, she realised, drawing her inexorably into the web she'd known before.

Murmuring to her in his own language, he caressed her arms and the delicate curve of her shoulders, slipping down to probe beneath the hem of her tank-top.

His fingers lingered in the sensitive hollow of her spine, causing another shiver of awareness. Her flesh was filmed with dampness, her scent rising to his nostrils when he bent his head and licked her skin. But the waistband of her skirt was a barrier, and his hands slid along her thighs instead to where her legs were bared and accessible.

'*Aghapita,*' he breathed, bending his head to kiss the inner curve of her thigh. 'You are so beautiful!'

'Dear God, Demetri—don't!'

'I want to.'

He wouldn't listen to her protests, and Jane was finding it increasingly hard to hold on to her sanity. Besides, there was something enormously satisfying in hearing the break in his voice when he spoke to her, the raw emotion that no amount of arrogance could hide.

He spread her legs, his lips moving sensuously along her thigh, bestowing a trail of hot wet kisses that made her gulp and come half up out of the chair. 'Relax,' he said, pushing her down again. 'Just let me do this.'

It was insane, she thought. Didn't he care where he was, what might happen if his mother or Ariadne took it into their heads to come and see what was happening?

Evidently not. His mouth had reached the delta of her thighs and she felt his hands slip beneath her bottom and find the elasticated tape of her thong. Then, with a determination that no amount of resistance on her part could defeat, he pulled the scrap of silk away.

'That is much better,' he said thickly, lifting his head to

press a hungry kiss to her parted lips. She felt his finger probe the moist curls at the top of her legs. 'Isn't it?'

Jane couldn't speak. She could only move her head in a helpless gesture of admission. And, as if her flushed face and agitated reaction pleased him, Demetri gripped the back of her neck and brought her mouth to his again in a hard, passionate possession.

'*Se thelo,*' he groaned, and she thought it was an indication of how aroused he was that he continued to speak in his own language. 'I want you,' he repeated hoarsely. '*Angikse me!*' Touch me!

Her hands had been twisted together in her lap but now they moved almost of their own accord. With a feeling of inevitability, she clutched his shoulders, pushing his suit jacket to the floor.

Beneath his shirt, his skin was hot. His heat surged up into her fingers, almost burning her, and when he bore her back against the cushions she found he was sweating, too.

He pushed her tank-top up above her breasts, using his tongue and his teeth to bring them to tingling, sensual life. He drew the swollen nubs into his mouth, sucking hungrily, and, because her nipples were already tender, she couldn't deny the moan of anguish that escaped her.

But he wasn't hurting her. Indeed, she thought, she had never felt more excited. Her belief that a pregnant woman couldn't possibly respond in the same way as before simply wasn't true. Demetri had always been able to drive her crazy with longing and today was no exception.

She was aware of him unbuckling his belt and loosening the button at his waist and she couldn't resist. Pushing his fingers aside, she pressed his zip down and then caught her breath when his arousal pushed a handful of his silk boxer shorts into her hand. The boxers were made of the finest fabric but, when she peeled them over his erection, she had to admit that his skin was smoother and more satinlike than the richest velvet.

'*Theos*,' he said on a choked breath, and she realised how close to release he was.

'You like that?' she asked unsteadily, and he made a sound of pained submission.

'I like it,' he told her unevenly, and that was when she acknowledged that she wanted him just as much as he wanted her. Feeling his naked sex against hers, she knew the decision was no longer open to discussion. Even if she might regret it later—and she was fairly sure she would—there was nothing she wanted more.

'But we—we can't do it here,' she protested, aware that they were in full view of anybody walking past the window outside.

Demetri uttered a strangled groan. 'Don't you dare move,' he muttered, pushing her skirt up around her waist. 'This is good enough for me.'

And when Demetri pushed into her hot, slick sheath, she discovered she wasn't much interested in objecting again. He lifted her legs and encouraged her to wind them about his waist and then entered her in one smooth, satisfying lunge. He pressed in so deeply that Jane's body had to expand and stretch to accommodate him, but dear God, she thought, he made her feel whole again.

'*Aghapi mou*,' he whispered and, when she gasped, 'Am I hurting you?'

'You asked me that before,' she reminded him huskily, and he arched an anxious brow.

'Well?'

'No! God, no,' she assured him unsteadily, and, with a groan of satisfaction, Demetri looked down at where their bodies were joined.

'*Telios,*' he breathed. 'You are perfect. We are perfect together, *neh?*'

'*Neh.* I mean, yes, yes,' she got out with an effort. Then, half closing her eyes, 'Please: don't stop now.'

'I do not believe I could, *pethi mou,*' he confessed, and she was so wet, when he drew back she could hear the audible suction of his flesh against hers. 'There are limits to even my control, sweet one, and we passed them some minutes ago.' He pushed into her again and now he began to quicken his pace. '*Theos,* we belong together.'

Jane couldn't deny it. Not at that moment, not when her body convulsed around his only seconds before his release. She felt him spurting inside her, felt his heat melting all coherent thought, and clamped her thighs around him in a final act of possession.

She wasn't sure how long she lay there with Demetri cradled between her thighs. In the beginning, she couldn't have moved, and then she found she didn't want to. Their bodies were still joined and she knew it would take very little to arouse him again. His sex lay, still semi-aroused, in her, and she knew she had only to put down her hand and touch him to have him harden into desire.

But, eventually, she forced herself to raise her arm and look at her watch and saw to her horror that they'd been in the library for over an hour. Someone—probably his mother—was going to start wondering what was taking so long, and Jane could just imagine how she would react if she opened the door and found her precious son half-naked in his soon-to-be-ex-wife's arms.

It was that awareness as much as anything that made her struggle to get free. She couldn't bear the thought that Maria Souvakis might witness her humiliation. For, however she tried to interpret it, the fact remained that once again she'd allowed Demetri to take advantage of her. Heavens, hadn't she learned her lesson the first time? She was pregnant, for goodness' sake. And she hadn't got that way by any immaculate conception.

'*Komatia,* what are you doing?'

Demetri's lazy protest caused her to quicken her actions. And because he was still semi-comatose, she was able to push him aside and scramble off the chair.

'I'm leaving,' she said unsteadily, tugging her tank down over her breasts and snatching up her underwear, which she stuffed into the pocket of her skirt. She averted her eyes from his shameless nakedness. 'If I were you, I'd put your clothes on. I doubt if Ariadne would appreciate seeing you in your present state of undress.'

Demetri swore, but she noticed he did as she suggested, tugging up his trousers and fastening his zip. But when she thought it was safe to leave, he pushed himself up from the chair and regarded her through narrowed eyes.

'We're not through, you know,' he said harshly, and, although she only glanced in his direction, she knew she would never forget the sight of him with his shirt unfastened and his zip in definite danger of slipping open again.

'I think we are,' she retorted, and this time when she headed for the door he didn't try to stop her.

'I'll see you at dinner,' he said, and, although Jane badly wanted to deny this, she was a guest in his father's house and the decision wasn't hers to make.

Shaking her head, she let herself out of the door, praying that she'd be allowed to go to her room without meeting either Ariadne or Ianthe or some member of Demetri's family. She wanted to be alone, she wanted time to think, and most of all she wanted to escape this awful predicament she'd created for herself.

But that wasn't going to happen. And the idea of not having the baby was as painful to her as leaving the island was going to be. But she had to leave. And soon. Before she did something totally outrageous like telling Demetri she was going to have his baby. Ironically enough, it would have been easier to tell him she still loved him than that.

She caught her breath. Was that true? Could she have been foolish enough to fall in love with him all over again? Because whatever happened, Demetri was never going to believe she hadn't got pregnant deliberately, and did she really want a relationship based on that suspicion?

No, she had to leave here. Even if Demetri was prepared to believe her, there would always be the spectre of Ianthe's baby in the background. And he had a new relationship now, with Ariadne. She didn't have the right to disrupt his life again.

Even if he had disrupted hers...

She had reached the stairs when someone called her name. At first she thought it might be Demetri and she continued on her way. But then she realised that once again the voice had been too mild to be her husband's and, glancing back, she saw Leo leaning heavily on the banister below.

She halted immediately, supremely conscious that she was flushed and out of breath. But then, with a gesture of defeat, she came down the stairs again, hoping that the lowering sun would cast her face in shadow.

'I was just going to change,' she said when he didn't speak again, and Leo inclined his head.

'Ariadne told me that Demetri was with you,' he said at last. 'I hope he hasn't upset you again.'

Upset!

Jane felt a sob of hysteria rise in her throat and quickly fought it down. 'It—he just wanted to ask me if I'd received the divorce papers,' she said, which was true. Then, moistening her lips, she added, 'I'm glad I've got this opportunity to speak to you, actually, Leo. I think it's time I went back to England.'

Demetri's father frowned. 'You do?'

'Yes.' Jane swallowed. 'Now that Demetri's back—'

'So he has been intimidating you—'

'No.' Jane couldn't allow him to think that. 'It's just—well, I'm in the way here.'

'You're not in my way, Jane.'

'No, but you know what I'm saying.' Jane sighed. 'It's been wonderful seeing you again, Leo, but I don't belong here any more.'

Leo sighed. 'Well, if that's your decision…'

'It is.' And then, seeing his disappointment, Jane came right down the stairs to give him an impulsive hug. 'You know I don't want to leave you—'

'Then why do so?'

'I just have to,' she insisted, drawing back. 'Please say you understand.'

Leo shook his head. 'I assume you've told Demetri.'

'Um—not yet, no.'

'Don't you think he'll have something to say about it?'

'Perhaps.' Jane sighed. And then, because telling Demetri was something she couldn't face right now, she added, 'Would you do that, Leo? Tell him, I mean? But not—not before dinner, if you don't mind.'

Leo looked troubled. 'Are you afraid of him, Jane?'

'No.' Jane stifled a groan. 'I just—don't want any fuss,' she murmured awkwardly. 'And now, if you don't mind, I'd like to go and have a shower before we eat.'

CHAPTER ELEVEN

To DEMETRI'S relief, Thermia wasn't joining them for dinner. Only his parents, Stefan and Ariadne were waiting in the orangery when he arrived, and, although he wanted to ask where Jane was, in the circumstances he decided discretion was the better part of valour.

To begin with, his father detained him in conversation about the conference he'd been attending, but as soon as the old man paused to speak to Demetri's mother, Ariadne took his place.

'What on earth took you so long this afternoon?' she exclaimed. 'You and that woman were in the library for ages. I was forced to entertain your mother and your aunt, and believe me that wasn't easy.'

'Thermia's not my aunt,' said Demetri evenly. 'Did Ianthe come back?'

'No.' Ariadne showed her displeasure. 'Did you èxpect she would?'

'I hoped she wouldn't,' retorted Demetri tersely. 'Ianthe and I have nothing to say to one another.'

Ariadne looked pleased at this. 'I notice your wife didn't take kindly to seeing the two of you together,' she commented. 'I suppose it brings back too many unhappy memories, hmm?'

Demetri found it difficult to conceal his resentment now. 'What unhappy memories?' he demanded. 'Jane hardly knows Ianthe.'

'No.' Ariadne shrugged. 'But seeing Ianthe must remind her of how close the two of you used to be.'

'Jane and me?'

'No.' Ariadne clicked her tongue. 'You and Ianthe. Come on, Demetri. I know the child she had was yours.'

'You don't know anything of the kind.' Demetri spoke through his teeth. 'In any case, I'd prefer not to talk about it. To you or anyone else.'

'Oh, I see.' Ariadne's dark brows lifted in amusement. 'That's what you and Jane were arguing about, was it?' She gave a snort of satisfaction. 'I can imagine how pleasant that would be.'

Demetri was tempted to say she didn't know what she was talking about, but it was easier to let her believe that he and Jane had been arguing rather than have her speculate on what else they might have been doing. *Theos,* he thought incredulously. Had he really made love to Jane in full view of the library windows? What did she do to him to make him care so little about who might see them? And when was this mad infatuation going to end?

'Your mother will be glad to see the back of her,' Ariadne was continuing, unaware that she no longer had his undivided attention. 'And I think even Leo is beginning to wish he'd never invited her here.'

Demetri doubted that. Remembering the way his father had treated Jane that afternoon, he'd been left in no doubt that the old man was very fond of her. Too fond, perhaps, if he expected his son to divorce her and marry someone else.

A twinge of awareness made him turn towards the door just in time to see his father going to greet the woman in question. This evening Jane was wearing narrow-legged silk trousers and a wide-necked silk sweater, both in black, that accentuated the intense fairness of her skin.

The sweater had been designed to slip off one or both shoulders, revealing that its owner wasn't wearing a bra. And Demetri found himself remembering the paleness of her breasts against his hands, the rosy peaks that had tasted so sweet just a couple of hours ago…

The memory caused him to harden immediately and he wished he were wearing a jacket to hide the sudden constriction of his trousers. He consoled himself with the assurance that it was fairly dark in the orangery with only scattered lanterns to provide illumination. Besides, by the time his father was willing to relinquish her undivided attention and brought Jane to join the rest of the family he had himself in control again.

'Why don't you get your wife a drink, Demetri?' his father suggested half maliciously, and, although Demetri resented the familiarity, at least it gave him a reason to tear his eyes away from her.

'*Ouzo?*' he offered with what he considered was admirable tolerance, but Jane shook her head.

'Just orange juice, please,' she said, and he noticed she was avoiding his eyes, too. Then she turned to smile at his younger brother, who was lounging near by. 'Hey, Stefan, I forgot to thank you for taking me into Kalithi this morning. I do appreciate it.'

Stefan made some easy deprecatory comment, but Demetri could feel his hackles rising at the thought of Jane and his younger brother together. *Chesta,* Stefan wasn't supposed to care for the company of women. What the hell was he doing taking Jane into town? She could drive, couldn't she? Why didn't she just take herself?

In consequence, he made the mistake of looking at her when

he brought the glass of orange juice she'd requested and was rewarded by a decidedly provocative stare in return. 'Thanks,' she said. Then, as if she cared, 'Aren't you drinking this evening?'

Demetri's jaw tightened. 'I'm not in the mood,' he said, thinking privately that getting drunk might be precisely the right thing to do in his present state of mind. He arched a sardonic brow. 'So what did you buy in Kalithi? If I'd known you needed something, I could have arranged to bring it back from Athens.'

'Don't you know that a woman doesn't have to *need* anything to enjoy shopping?' Stefan interposed lightly. 'And you a married man and all.'

'Not for much longer,' put in Ariadne swiftly, not to be outdone. 'Isn't that right, darling?' She tucked her arm through Demetri's. 'You can't wait to be free.'

Demetri saw Jane press her lips together at this blatant piece of propaganda, but it was Stefan who answered for her. 'Then it's just as well I'm here to act as Jane's protector,' he remarked, slipping an arm about her waist and drawing her closer. 'We get along famously, don't we, darling?'

Jane's smile appeared again. 'Well, I must admit you've looked after me very well,' she agreed, and Demetri found himself wanting to push his fist into his brother's smug face.

'So why didn't you drive into town yourself?' he asked tersely, releasing himself from Ariadne's clinging hold. 'Your car's still in the garage, isn't it?'

'Oh, your mother's given the little Porsche to me, Demetri.' Ariadne tried to capture his arm again, but he shook her off. 'And Jane doesn't live here any more—'

'My mother had no right to give that car to anyone,' retorted Demetri furiously, and even Stefan looked surprised at his vehemence.

'It's not as if it was a new car,' he ventured, but one look at his brother's face made him bite his tongue.

'The car belongs to Jane,' insisted Demetri harshly, and now even Ariadne looked put out. '*Hristo,* why wasn't I consulted about this?'

Maria Souvakis had heard the raised voices and now she turned to look disapprovingly at her eldest son. 'For heaven's sake, Demetri, it's just a car, you know. Not the crown jewels!'

'And you couldn't wait to humiliate Jane, could you?' he snapped angrily. He turned to look at Ariadne. 'Don't tell me you went to pick her up from the ferry in the Porsche!'

'Of course I did.' It was obvious Ariadne didn't understand what all the fuss was about. 'As your mother says, it is only a car, Demetri.'

'It's Jane's car, not yours,' he returned bleakly, and now Jane knew she had to intervene before he said or did something he would definitely regret after she'd gone.

'I don't want it,' she said, meeting his incensed gaze with cool deliberation. 'Ariadne's welcome to it.' Her lips twisted. 'It goes with the territory.'

'If you think—'

Jane had no idea what Demetri might have said then had not his father called a halt to the argument. 'Dinner is served,' he told them all severely. 'Angelena has been trying to attract our attention for the past five minutes.' He gave Demetri a warning look. 'Shall we go in?'

The meal itself was something of an anticlimax. Grilled aubergines were followed by a Greek salad with *psaria* as the main course. The latter was a whole fish, baked with vegetables and served in a tomato, fennel and olive-oil sauce. It was very spicy, and probably delicious, but Jane, whose uncertain constitution hadn't been improved by the earlier altercation, found it all rather rich for her taste. She was grateful when the plates were removed and the dessert was served. The sweet flaky pastries were much more to her liking.

She didn't think anyone had noticed her lack of appetite, but when they left the table to go into the adjoining salon for coffee, she found Demetri at her side.

'Not hungry?' he asked in an undertone, and she permitted herself an impatient look in his direction.

'Are you surprised?'

'You're blaming me?'

'Well, I have to wonder what all that excessive outrage was about. You're going to marry Ariadne. Why shouldn't she have use of the car?'

Demetri's nostrils flared. 'It means that little to you?'

'Demetri, it's probably been standing idle for the last five years. Why not?'

'I've had it serviced regularly.'

'Good for you.'

Jane tried to sound indifferent, but his persistence was telling on her nerves. It was devastating to be this close to him physically, yet be aware of the gulf between them. Her mind was filled with what had happened that afternoon and she hated it that he seemed so totally removed now from that flagrant intimacy.

Demetri scowled. 'I suppose that's why you asked Stefan to take you into town,' he said harshly. 'I didn't know you and my brother were such good friends.'

'There's a lot of things you don't know about your brother,' retorted Jane shortly, and then wished she could control her impulsive tongue. She glanced quickly about the room and saw that the rest of the family were waiting for them to join them. 'We ought to sit down.'

'In a second.'

Fortunately the maid chose that moment to appear with the coffee-pot. And, although Jane was sure that both Maria and Ariadne were cursing the screen she created between them, it did allow Demetri the time to demand that she explain what she meant.

'It's not important,' she insisted, wishing she could retract her words. 'Look, your mother and Ariadne are watching us.'

'I want to know what you meant.' Demetri was insistent. 'What don't I know about Stefan? Don't tell me he's had a sudden epiphany; that he's decided he prefers women to men, after all?'

'Don't be so patronising.' Jane bitterly resented his attitude. 'Apparently Stefan and his partner have been together over six years.'

'I did know that.' Demetri lifted his shoulders. 'They have a house in Kalithi. Stefan's only spending so much time at the villa because of our father's illness.'

'That's right.' Jane was aware that all eyes were on them now. 'So there you are, then.'

Demetri's scowl deepened. 'You still haven't explained what you meant about Stefan. What don't I know that I should?'

'Oh, Demetri…' Jane sighed. 'We can't discuss it now.'

'Very well.' He inclined his head. 'I'll come to your room later. You can tell me then.'

Jane couldn't resist it. 'Won't you be with Ariadne?' she asked innocently, and was glad his family's presence prevented him from making the kind of response she deserved.

'After this afternoon?' he countered. 'I don't think so.'

'Oh, Demetri.' A sob of hysteria rose inside her and, to disguise her real feelings, she said recklessly, 'You must be getting old. When we were together, you used to have much more stamina.'

A phone rang somewhere in the house, but Demetri ignored it. He was staring at Jane with undisguised fury in his eyes, and she hastily moved around a sofa to seat herself beside his father. She knew it wasn't fair to provoke him when he couldn't answer back, but this time it seemed she'd gone too far, even for him.

'What the hell is that supposed to mean?' he demanded, coming to grip the back of the sofa behind her with white-knuckled fingers. 'Jane, I'm warning you—'

But whatever he'd been about to reveal was arrested by the sudden appearance of his father's housekeeper. Angelena halted in the doorway, and it was obvious from her flushed face and agitated hands that she had something momentous to report.

'My apologies, *kirie,*' she said, looking at Demetri, 'but you have a call from Athens.' She spoke in their own language but Jane could understand most of what she said. 'I explained that the family was at dinner, but Kirie Avensis insists on speaking to you personally. He says it is a matter of life and death!'

Demetri hesitated only a moment before turning and following the woman out of the room. His departure left an uncomfortable vacuum, which Leo filled with his usual aptitude.

'Avensis wouldn't ring unless it was something serious,' he averred half rising out of his seat and then sinking weakly back again. 'Maria, would you go and see what has happened? I would myself, but...'

He spread his hands, his meaning clear, and for once Maria didn't demur. '*Veveha,*' she said, putting down her coffee and getting to her feet. Of course. 'If you will all excuse me...'

Jane didn't know what to say, but Stefan had no such reservations. 'You could have asked me, Papa,' he said tersely. 'I am capable of carrying a message, you know.'

Leo shook his head, for once looking less than self-possessed. 'I didn't think, Stefan. I'm sorry. And of course you may go and see if there is anything you can do.'

Stefan shook his head. 'Is there any point?'

'There may be.' His father's face had resumed its normal composure. 'If you wouldn't mind.'

Stefan hesitated, but after a moment, he, too, got to his feet and left the room, leaving Demetri's father with only Jane and Ariadne for company.

'What do you think has happened?'

Ariadne voiced what they were all thinking, and Leo shook his head again. 'Heaven knows,' he said, his fingers massaging the head of his cane his only sign of agitation. 'One of the tankers has had a collision, perhaps.'

Ariadne's lips parted. 'Is that serious?'

'It can be.' Leo forced a smile for their benefit. 'Let us hope not, hmm?'

Jane wet her dry lips. 'Will—will Demetri be expected to take charge?'

'Not necessarily,' replied the old man, before Ariadne could tell her it was none of her business. He stared thoughtfully into the middle distance. 'We have technical staff for that sort of thing.' He paused. 'Of course, he may want to.'

'As you would,' said Jane understandingly, and Leo smiled a little wistfully.

'You know me so well, my dear,' he said, patting her hand. 'Yes. I would love to be involved.'

Jane smiled and Ariadne huffed her annoyance, but just then Maria came back into the room, adjusting her grave expression when she saw her husband.

'Well?' Leo was impatient, and Maria sighed.

'There's been an accident,' she said, sinking down onto her

chair again and lifting her cooling cup of coffee. 'Ugh, where's Angelena? This is barely palatable—'

'What kind of accident?'

Leo wasn't about to be put off, and Maria put her cup down again. 'Demetri will handle it,' she said soothingly. 'Now, does anyone else—?'

'Maria!' Leo was glaring at her now, and, with a groan, she gave in.

'All right, all right. There's been an explosion. It's not clear yet how it happened, but the *Artemis* is holed just above the waterline.'

Leo swore then. 'Holed?' he echoed. 'Has anyone been hurt?'

'Avensis says one man has been reported injured, but other than that there are no casualties.'

'Thank God!' Leo was relieved. 'But the *Artemis*: is she in danger of sinking?'

'Possibly.' Maria leant towards him and rubbed his knee. 'It's nothing for you to worry about, Leo. As I said before, Demetri will handle it.'

Leo's frustration was evident. 'I assume he's flying back to Athens tonight?'

'He's arranging to have Costas pick him up as we speak,' agreed Maria reassuringly.

'Yes.' Leo nodded. 'The helicopter will allow him to fly straight out to the stricken vessel.'

'Oh, I shouldn't think so.' Now his wife looked dismayed and Jane felt a stab of anxiety deep inside her.

'Oh, yes.' Leo sounded definite. 'I know Demetri. He'll want to see for himself what is going on.'

'But—isn't that dangerous?'

It was Ariadne who spoke now, and Demetri's father gave her an impatient look. 'Life is dangerous,' he muttered.

'Haven't you discovered that yet?' His lips twisted. 'Jane has, haven't you, my dear?'

Jane didn't know what to say to this, but, as luck would have it, Stefan's return prevented any need for a reply.

'Has Mama told you what's happened, Papa?' he asked, leaning over the sofa where they were sitting. And at Leo's nod, 'I'm going with Demetri.' He arched mocking brows at Jane. 'Ain't that somethin'?'

Jane could only stare at him, and it was left to Maria to say anxiously, 'You can't both be going, Stefan. What about— what about your father? What about us? We may need you—'

'Let him go, Maria,' Leo interrupted her. 'Perhaps it's time I remembered I had three sons and not just two, eh, Stefan?' He paused. 'Just be careful, hmm?'

'I will, Papa.' Stefan gripped the old man's shoulder for a moment, and then, after bidding goodbye to the three women, he left the room again.

Maria looked near to tears and Jane herself felt decidedly shaken. The idea of the two men flying out to some oil tanker that had already experienced one explosion was terrifying. She wanted to go and find Demetri and tell him to take care, but she didn't have that right, and it was Ariadne who, after a moment, sprang to her feet and followed Stefan.

'Well!' Maria regarded Jane coldly. 'I hope you won't let this interfere with your plans for leaving.' She paused and ignoring her husband's obvious dismay, she continued, 'Leo tells me you want to leave as soon as possible. In the circumstances, I think that's entirely the right thing to do. Don't you?'

CHAPTER TWELVE

JANE parked her car outside her mother's house and then sat for a few moments wondering how she was going to handle this. She had to tell her mother she was going to have a baby. She couldn't take the risk that Olga might decide to make her suspicions public. Besides, she hadn't seen Mrs Lang for over a week and her mother deserved to know the truth.

Nevertheless, she wasn't looking forward to telling her who the baby's father was. After everything that had happened, the words *'I told you so'* were bound to make an appearance, and she had had enough of feeling like a pariah.

She'd left Kalithi the previous afternoon. Despite his reluctance to see her leave, Demetri's father had arranged for a helicopter to take her to Athens instead of Andros, where a first-class air ticket back to London had been waiting for her.

Jane had been very grateful, even if Demetri's mother hadn't approved. She'd slept badly the night before she left, not knowing where Demetri was or what he was doing. She couldn't deny the fears she had for both his and Stefan's safety, and if Maria hadn't made her position so impossible she might have stayed for a couple of days longer, just to assure herself that all was well.

In the event, Leo had assured her that he'd had word from

Demetri and that the news was good, but that wasn't the same as hearing it for herself. And Leo was going to be here, at the epicentre of all information, while back home in London, Jane would have to rely on the news channels for any word about the *Artemis*. And her husband.

Leo had accompanied her to the helicopter pad and said his goodbyes there, far from his wife's disapproving gaze. He'd thanked her again for coming, had expressed the wish that perhaps they'd meet again, and Jane had told him that, any time he wanted to see her, he had only to let her know.

Which had perhaps not been the wisest thing to say, in the circumstances, she acknowledged. How could she return to Kalithi when in a matter of weeks, possibly less, her condition was going to be obvious?

Still, it was unlikely to happen, she thought, feeling a twinge of despair at the thought of never seeing Demetri's father again. While they'd waited for the pilot to load her luggage, she'd got the feeling that there'd been so much more he'd wanted to say to her. She guessed he'd wanted to defend his son, but he hadn't been able to find the words.

Now, however, she had to put those days on Kalithi behind her. Her life was here, in London, and in a matter of days she would have to re-immerse herself in the business of buying and selling art and antiques. She owed it to Olga. She owed it to herself.

Mrs Lang opened the door as Jane walked up the garden path. 'Well, well!' she exclaimed, accepting her daughter's kiss before stepping back to allow her to enter the narrow hall of the townhouse. 'You didn't let me know you were back.'

'I got home last night,' said Jane, gesturing towards the kitchen at the back of the house. 'Shall we just sit in here?'

'No, we'll go upstairs.' Apart from the kitchen and a

second bathroom, all the living quarters were on the first and second floors. 'I've just made a pot of tea. You go ahead. I'll get the tray.'

Jane hesitated. 'Do you need any help?'

'I'm quite capable of carrying a tray upstairs,' retorted Mrs Lang tartly. 'I'll just be a minute.'

'OK.'

With a shrug, Jane climbed the stairs and entered her mother's living room, which overlooked the front of the house. Polished cabinets, occasional tables covered with an assortment of knick-knacks, and a neat three-piece suite. There was patterned broadloom on the floor, and lace curtains at the windows, and Jane couldn't help comparing it to the almost spartan appearance of her own apartment.

No wonder Mrs Lang didn't encourage Lucy and her brood to visit, she thought drily, trying to distract herself. Paul and Jessica couldn't help but create havoc here.

'Sit down, for goodness' sake!'

Her mother had appeared in the doorway and now she came bustling into the room to set the tray she was carrying on the low table in front of the hearth. It was warm enough outside not to need the gas fire today, but Jane could tell from the heat of the room that her mother had had the radiators on.

She seated herself in one of the armchairs, accepting the cup of tea her mother handed her. 'Thanks,' she said, grateful it wasn't coffee. She still couldn't face that on an empty stomach.

'So, there we are.' Mrs Lang perched on the sofa close by. 'This is cosy, isn't it?' Then she gave her daughter an appraising stare. 'But you're still looking peaky. Do I take it, it didn't go well?'

'It—went OK.' Jane was vague. 'Leo made me very welcome.'

'What about Demetri? Was he there?' Then she frowned. 'That reminds me: there was something about a tanker of his

catching fire. It was on the TV this morning. In the Mediterranean, I think. I don't suppose you know anything about that?'

Jane caught her breath. 'What did they say? Has—has
anyone been hurt?'

Her mother's frown deepened. 'If you mean was Demetri
mentioned, then no. Obviously, he wouldn't be. Men like him
don't get involved in minor incidents like explosions!'

'That's not true.' Jane couldn't let her get away with such a
statement. 'As a matter of fact, I did know about the accident.
It happened the night before I came home. Both Demetri and
his brother left for Athens immediately.'

'So is that why you came home?'

'No!' Jane was defensive. 'I'd already told Leo I was leaving
before it happened.'

'Oh, well…' Her mother sniffed and took a sip of her tea
before continuing, 'From what I heard, it wasn't much of a fire.
I suppose it made news because of the danger it could have
posed to other vessels.'

Jane nodded, not trusting herself to speak about it. It wasn't
the danger the tanker had posed to other vessels that had
alarmed her. Simply knowing her husband was involved had
been enough.

There was silence for a few moments and then Mrs Lang
said, 'And how was Mr Souvakis?'

'Oh—not too bad. Very thin, of course, and he doesn't have
a lot of strength. But his mind's still as active as ever.'

'Do you really think so?' Her mother sounded sceptical.

'What do you mean?'

'Well, he knows you and Demetri are getting a divorce,
doesn't he? So he must have known it wasn't the wisest thing,
inviting you out there. Surely he didn't think that bringing you
two together might cause a change of heart?'

'No.' Jane's hand trembled and she quickly replaced her cup and saucer on the tray. 'No, of course not.'

Her mother studied her thoughtfully. 'Did you?' she asked shrewdly and Jane felt the hot colour flood her cheeks.

'Did I what?'

'Hope that Demetri might change his mind?'

'No!' And it was true. When she'd left England, she hadn't hoped for any such thing. 'I—I left Demetri, Mum. Not the other way about.'

'Hmm.' Mrs Lang didn't look convinced, and Jane thought how impossible it was going to be to tell her about the baby now. 'So when are you going back to work?'

Jane expelled a weary breath. 'I don't know. Tomorrow. The day after. I'll speak to Olga.'

Her mother huffed. 'How nice to be so blasé about it.'

Jane moistened her lips. 'Well—I haven't been feeling all that good, actually.'

'Ah, I thought so.' Mrs Lang looked triumphant. 'I told you, you looked ill before you went away.'

'So you did.' Jane felt a sense of resignation.

'What is it, then? Have you been to see a doctor?'

'I went before I went away.'

'And you never said a word.' Her mother looked offended. 'I suppose you told that Ivanovitch woman what you were doing. You tell her everything. But I'm just your mother. You don't think I deserve to know what's going on—'

'I'm pregnant!'

Jane hadn't known what she was going to say until the words were spoken. She just knew she had to stop her mother making claims that simply weren't true. But afterwards, she just sat and stared at her with horrified eyes.

This time the silence was longer. Her mother put down her

own cup almost unthinkingly, swallowing several times as if her throat was suddenly very dry.

Then she said quietly, 'It's Demetri's, I suppose.'

Jane's shoulders sagged. 'Yes.'

'Oh, Jane!' She'd expected many things from her mother, but not sympathy. 'How long have you known? Is this why you really went out to Greece?'

'No!' Jane shook her head. 'Demetri doesn't know. He mustn't know. He's going to marry someone else.'

Her mother stared at her in disbelief. 'You're not serious!'

'I am.'

'But Jane, how can you let him marry someone else when you're expecting his child? You're not making any sense.'

Jane sighed. 'Mum, my being pregnant makes no difference to—to our feelings for one another.'

'I can't believe that.'

Jane bit her lip. 'What happened between Demetri and me was—a mistake. It should never have happened.'

'So why did it?'

'Oh, I don't know.' Jane was glad now she hadn't told her mother why Demetri wanted a divorce. 'I was—upset, and he—he—'

'Took advantage of you.'

'No, it wasn't like that.'

'So what was it like?'

Jane felt the colour enter her cheeks at the question. 'Mum, please. It happened. Can't you just accept that?'

Her mother looked at her closely. 'Don't you usually take precautions on—on occasions like this?'

'I don't usually have occasions like this,' replied Jane honestly. 'It was reckless, I know. But my period was due and—'

'And you thought you'd be OK?'

'Yes.'

'Dear lord!'

'I know. It was stupid. I realise that now.'

'I wonder how many young women have said that.' Mrs Lang got up from the sofa to pace restlessly about the room. 'And let's face it, he's just as much to blame.'

'He probably thought the same as you: that I'd take care of it.' She shrugged. 'It wasn't something we discussed at the time.'

'Even so—'

'Mum, this isn't Demetri's problem. It's mine. And I want to keep it that way.'

'Humph.' Her mother snorted. 'That man seems to make a habit of fathering children with women he shouldn't.' She hesitated. 'I assume you saw—what was her name?—Ianthe, while you were there.'

Jane bent her head. 'I saw her, yes.'

'And is that who he's going to marry?'

'No.' Jane hesitated. Then she said, 'Ianthe's baby died.'

Her mother's brows ascended. 'Really? How convenient!'

'It wasn't like that.' Jane had to defend the other girl. 'I believe she was very upset.'

'And was Demetri upset, too?'

'I think so.' She paused and then added, 'He still maintains the baby wasn't his.'

Mrs Lang stared at her. 'You don't believe him, do you?'

Jane made a helpless gesture. 'N...o.'

'That's something, anyway.' Her mother's face mirrored her relief. 'So what do you plan to do? Bring up the child yourself?'

'That's one option, obviously.'

'One option?' Mrs Lang frowned. 'What other options have you got? If you're not going to involve Demetri...' The words trailed away and, when she spoke again, there was real concern in her voice. 'You wouldn't consider not—not having the baby, would you? I mean,' she rushed on, 'there's no need for any hasty decisions. I'd be happy to do what I can and I know Lucy would help out.'

'Oh, Mum!' Jane felt her eyes fill with tears. 'The last thing you need is a baby here.'

'If it makes the difference between you having the baby and not, there's no argument,' retorted her mother firmly. She glanced about the cluttered room with impatient eyes. 'It's time I had a clear-out. Lucy's always telling me that. And don't forget, that baby's my grandchild, just as much as Paul and Jessica.'

'Oh, Mum,' said Jane chokily, getting up and enfolding the older woman in her arms. 'I do love you, you know.'

'I should hope you do.' Mrs Lang tried to sound indignant and didn't quite make it. 'Now drink your tea. Pregnant young women need to keep their strength up.'

CHAPTER THIRTEEN

DEMETRI was standing at the bedroom window of his house in Kalithi, staring out at the darkening ocean, when there was a tentative knock at his door.

Cursing, because he hadn't yet started to dress for dinner at the villa, he went to open it, hoping against hope that it wasn't Ariadne. He could do without another argument with her, he thought heavily. She couldn't understand why he hadn't been to her bed since seeing his estranged wife again. And God knew, he didn't have an answer for her.

But to his relief, it wasn't Ariadne. A manservant stood outside with the news that his father was waiting to see him. *His father?* Demetri didn't hesitate before following the man downstairs.

'Papa,' he said with some concern, entering the salon where the old man was reclining with evident relief on an ivory velvet sofa. 'Don't tell me you've driven here by yourself.'

'No, no.' Leo Souvakis regarded his eldest son with a mixture of affection and impatience. 'Micah brought me.' He paused. 'Though I have to say, I'm still capable of handling a motor vehicle.'

'If you say so.' Demetri slipped his hands into the pockets of his khaki shorts. But, although he adopted a conciliatory tone, he was well aware that his father's face showed the strain of walking unaided from the car into the house. 'Can I offer you a drink? Some wine, perhaps?'

Leo grimaced. 'Wine,' he muttered irritably.

'*Ouzo,* then.' Demetri walked across to the wet bar and returned a few moments later with an *ouzo* and water, the ice clinking pleasantly in the glass. 'Does that suit you better?'

'Much.' Leo took the glass and looked up at his son with a rueful expression on his face. 'You know your mother forbids me to drink this.' He took a taste, savouring the flavour of aniseed on his tongue. 'But I say, if I'm dying, why prolong the exercise?'

'You don't mean that.' Demetri dropped into the chair opposite his father, legs spread, clasped hands hanging between his knees. 'But I doubt if one rather weak drink is going to do you any harm.'

'Weak, eh?' Leo raised the glass to look into it, and then, seeing his son's face, he smiled. 'OK, I know I should be grateful. And I am. But every now and then…'

Demetri nodded. And then, because he knew the old man wouldn't have come here if he didn't have something on his mind, he said, 'So—what brings you here? Is something wrong?'

'You tell me.' Leo took another sip of the *ouzo,* regarding his son over the rim of the glass. 'Hmm, this is delicious, weak or otherwise.'

Demetri frowned, not diverted by the compliment. 'What is it you want me to tell you?'

'Oh, come on.' His father waited and, when his son didn't speak, he went on, 'Ariadne thinks you've changed your mind about getting married again. Or so she's informed your mother.'

Demetri felt the hot colour invade his face. 'Ariadne should keep her opinions to herself.'

'So it's not true?'

'That I've changed my mind about marrying her?' Demetri was defensive. 'I haven't said anything like that.'

'Or *done* anything?' suggested his father drily. 'How shall I put it? Ariadne is feeling—neglected, no?'

Demetri pushed himself to his feet. 'For pity's sake, what has she been saying?'

'I think I do not need to answer that, Demetri.'

His son groaned. 'God!'

'And if you're about to say it's got nothing to do with me, don't!' Leo looked up at him with shrewd eyes. 'Just answer me this: have you seen Jane since she went back to England?'

Demetri's jaw dropped. 'You know I haven't.'

'Do I?'

'You should. I've spent the last three weeks in Athens, dealing with the fallout from the explosion on the *Artemis*, if you'll excuse the pun. When have I had time to go to England?'

'And she hasn't visited you in Athens?'

'Who? Jane?' Demetri snorted. 'Of course not.'

'Well, if you tell me you haven't seen her, I have to believe you.' Leo took another mouthful of the *ouzo*. 'But tell me something else: have you wanted to?'

'Wanted to what?'

'See her, Demetri? See Jane? It's a simple enough question.'

Demetri swore then, pushing the chair he'd been occupying aside and striding across to the bar. Snatching up a bottle of single malt, he poured himself a stiff whisky, swallowing half of it in a gulp before turning to look at his father again.

'OK,' he said at last, raking an impatient hand over his scalp. 'Let's cut to the chase, shall we? What do you want me to say, Pa? Just tell me what you want to hear and I'll say it. That way I think we'll save a hell of a lot of time.'

Leo's mouth tightened. 'There's no need for this, Demetri. I asked you a simple question.'

'Yeah, right.'

'And I must assume from your reluctance to give me a simple answer that my concerns are justified.'

'No. No, they're not.' Demetri spoke heatedly. 'I admit, I haven't given Ariadne the attention she deserves in recent weeks, but as soon as the divorce is finalised, I'll be free to make up for it. You'll see.'

His father didn't look convinced. 'So seeing Jane again didn't make any difference to your feelings for Ariadne?'

'No!'

Leo sighed. 'Why don't I believe you?'

'Pa, how ever I feel—and I'm not saying I feel anything—Jane isn't interested in me. You know that.' He hesitated and, when his father's expression didn't change, he said doggedly, 'OK. There's a physical attraction between us. There always has been. But she's never going to forgive me for what she thinks I did to Ianthe. And nothing's going to alter that, so—'

'You could tell her the truth.'

'You think she'd believe me? She never has before.'

'That's because you've always kept something back.'

'Yes, and if she'd loved me she'd have believed me, whatever I said.'

'Oh, Demetri, don't be such a prig! How would you have felt if you'd discovered Jane was expecting a child and another man maintained he was the father?'

Demetri looked down into his glass. 'I hope I'd have given her the benefit of the doubt.'

'How gallant!' Leo was scornful. 'Demetri, I know you. You'd have kicked her out and then you'd have torn the other man apart.'

Demetri grunted. 'That's some opinion you have of me, Pa.' He paused. 'So what are you saying? That I shouldn't divorce Jane, after all?' He frowned. 'I thought you were fond of Ariadne.'

'I am fond of Ariadne.' His father was impatient. 'And when you were younger, I used to think she'd make you a good wife.' He shrugged. 'But it never happened. 'You met Jane, and I knew from the moment I saw you two together that she was the one love of your life.'

Demetri's jaw hardened. 'That was pretty fanciful, wasn't it? We didn't even like one another when we first met.'

'You may not have liked one another, but you certainly struck sparks off one another,' remarked Leo reflectively. 'You were so sure when you walked into the gallery that she was only stringing me a line.'

'Mmm.'

Demetri didn't want to remember how it had been, but he couldn't help the memories from flooding back. Finding his father discussing art with a girl who didn't look old enough to have left school, let alone be the possessor of an arts degree, had infuriated him.

Though he'd soon realised that his fury was directed towards his father as much as anyone else. Had he been jealous? He supposed he had. He'd certainly resented the fact that the old man had apparently found himself such a young and sexy companion. And when Leo had suggested that she deliver the delicate bronze he'd chosen to his hotel herself, Demetri had swiftly intervened.

He'd offered to collect the sculpture instead. There was no need for Ms Lang to put herself out, he'd said. He'd be passing the gallery again before he left England and he'd be happy to attend to the delivery personally.

Of course, she'd protested that it was no trouble, no trouble at all, and Demetri had been sure that that old harridan, Olga Ivanovitch, had been listening to their conversation and had had her own opinion of why he should want to cut his father out.

But, in the event, it was his father who'd made the decision. Smiling a little smugly, he'd agreed that that was probably the best solution, and consequently, a few days later, Demetri had called at the gallery to collect the purchase…

The gallery had appeared to be on the point of closing, he remembered. Long canvas shades had been drawn down and, when he'd opened the door, he'd half suspected the place was deserted. But then Jane had appeared from the office at the back of the showroom, and his pheromones had kicked into overdrive.

'I'm afraid we're closed—' she was beginning, when she recognised him. 'Oh, it's you!'

'*Neh,* me,' he agreed a little tersely. 'You were expecting me, I think. Did not my assistant warn you I was coming?'

'Warn me?' Green eyes sparkled and a look of amusement crossed her face. 'Are you a dangerous man, Mr Souvakis?'

'No, just an impatient one.' Demetri scowled, annoyed that she'd already put him on the defensive. 'The sculpture— it is ready?'

Her sigh was telling and he felt like an oaf for being so ill-mannered. 'It's ready,' she conceded, gesturing towards the office behind her. 'It's through here. If you'd like to come with me, I'll get your receipt.

'*Efkaristo.*'

He was unnecessarily brusque and he didn't know why. It wasn't as if she'd been particularly flippant. He knew she'd only been trying to be friendly, and he couldn't understand what it was about her that was causing him to behave so badly.

The office was small, just a couple of filing cabinets against the far wall, a computer and a printer, and a desk that was presently covered with black plastic bags.

'Sorry about this,' she said, indicating the bags. 'I've been having a clear-out and I haven't had time to dump these out the back yet.' She shoved some papers off a chair. 'Why don't you sit down? While I try and locate that receipt.'

Demetri paused in the doorway. She was obviously run off her feet and he wasn't making life any easier for her by treating her like an inferior.

Coming to an impulsive decision, he came into the room and hefted half a dozen of the plastic bags. 'Why don't you show me where you want these putting and then you'll have room to move around, *neh?*'

Her eyes widened in surprise and, when she smiled, he was struck by her sudden beauty. He'd already acknowledged that she was an attractive young woman, but, with faint colour giving her cheeks a dusky glow and her mouth with its fuller lower lip parted to reveal the pink tip of her tongue, she was stunning.

'Oh—that's very kind of you,' she began. 'But those bags are dusty. You might stain your suit.'

'Don't worry about it, *thespinis,*' he said, oblivious to the fact that his suit was pale grey and an Armani. 'Out the back, you said?'

'Yes.'

She stared at him for a moment longer, and then, apparently deciding he meant what he said, she came round the desk again and brushed past him on her way to the door.

It was just the briefest of contacts, but he was aware of her in a way he'd never been aware of a woman before. The slenderness of her body enchanted him and, in the somewhat humid confines of the office, her womanly scent caused a sharp rush of heat to his groin.

But then she was past him and out in the narrow passageway that led to the back of the building. She opened the door and he saw other bags already stacked outside.

'Just leave them here,' she said, stepping out of the way so he could drop his burden. 'They'll be collected later.' She smiled again. 'Thanks. I do appreciate it.'

'*Efkaristisi mou,*' he said. And when she looked blank, he translated, 'My pleasure.'

Jane waited until he'd passed through the door again, before shutting and locking it. 'Well, you must be very strong,' she murmured, and for the first time she made him smile.

'*Ineh poli evyeniko,*' he told her drily. 'You're very kind. I don't often get compliments like that.'

He could have added that he couldn't remember the last time he'd done any manual labour, but that would have sounded like boasting. Instead, he contented himself with brushing a hand down the front of his suit, pulling a wry face at the smear of dirt that resisted all his efforts to remove it.

'I'm sure you get plenty of compliments,' she retorted, apparently not convinced by his denial, going ahead of him along the hall, giving him an uninterrupted view of her back.

Firm shoulders, a narrow waist, a slim yet shapely rear. And long legs, shown to advantage in the short-skirted mini-dress she was wearing. Her hair, which she'd had secured in a pony-tail the first time he'd seen her, now hung in honey-streaked waves to her shoulder blades, and he knew a sudden urge to grab a handful and bury his face in its silky mass.

Forcing such thoughts aside, he found himself wondering if she had a date with some man this evening. Was that why she was wearing a dress that was so obviously unsuitable for the job she was doing? The last time he'd seen her, she'd been severely attired in a white blouse and a tailored skirt, and, although he'd noticed her legs, he couldn't remember seeing so much of them...

Dammit!

Dragging his thoughts out of the gutter, he saw they were back at the office and Jane was already opening drawers in the desk. 'It has to be here somewhere,' she was muttering to herself, and, pausing in the doorway, Demetri treated himself to the pleasure of just watching her. She was so lovely, so feminine, and it was many weeks since he'd had a woman in his bed.

Once again, he forced his eyes away from her. For heaven's sake, he chided himself, what was wrong with him? His father wasn't here now, so he couldn't excuse his behaviour on the grounds of provoking the old man. And it wasn't as if there was any shortage of women in his life. Being a wealthy man in his own right, and Leonides Souvakis' heir, opened many bedroom doors.

Of course, Jane was totally unaware of what he was thinking. She had no idea that images of her, spread-eagled beneath him, were occupying his thoughts. Thankfully, she couldn't read his mind or she wouldn't be bending over her desk like that, giving him a tantalising glimpse of her small, but very provocative, breasts.

'Where on earth can it be?' she was asking, but she was talking to herself, not to him. She pulled open the drawers again, one after the other, riffling through their contents with unflattering haste. It was obvious she wanted rid of him and that was a novelty in itself. 'It's got to be here somewhere. Olga gave it to me before she left. Just after—just after that person from your office phoned. I was sure I'd put it—ouch!'

Her cry of pain interrupted her and Demetri, who was still standing in the doorway, now came swiftly round the desk to her side. 'What have you done?'

There was blood on her finger and, without even thinking about it, he brought her hand to his mouth. He'd licked the wound clean before he realised she was gazing up at him with startled eyes, and he knew it was far too late to pretend ignorance of how his action might be interpreted.

'*Signomi*,' he said at once. 'I'm sorry. I shouldn't have done that.'

'No, you shouldn't.' She was indignant and it was painfully apparent that she didn't welcome the intimacy. 'It was stupid of me to make a fuss. It's only a paper cut.' She drew her fingers away and examined the injury for herself. 'I'll put a plaster on it and it'll be fine.'

Demetri inclined his head, stepping back to allow her to take what was apparently her handbag from a drawer of the filing cabinet and search it for plasters. A film of moisture appeared on her upper lip as she did so and he wondered if she was quite as indifferent to him as she'd have him believe.

Whatever, he chided himself, he hadn't come here to start an affair with the woman. He'd only been trying to protect his father's interests, that was all.

But that was such a lie! He had wanted to see her again. He might as well admit it. And that was when he'd thought she was a buttoned-up art student. Now, in feminine clothes and with an attitude he could cut with a knife, she was absolutely fascinating.

She'd found a plaster and, after discovering he was still watching her, she offered him a tight smile. 'I'm always getting paper cuts,' she said, peeling off the protective covering and attempting to apply the plaster to her finger. 'I sometimes think I should wear rubber gloves.'

'And hide those pretty hands?' Demetri shook his head and then, risking another rebuke, he took the plaster from her. '*Etho,* let me,' he said softly, using both hands to accomplish his task. He smoothed the plaster around her finger and smiled in satisfaction. '*Poli kalitera.* Much better, no?'

Jane looked down at their joined hands and then gave a

helpless little shrug. 'Yes. Thank you.' She blew out a nervous breath. 'Now, if you'll let me go, I'll get your package.'

Demetri's eyes held hers for a long, loaded moment before his hand fell to his side. 'If that's what you want, of course.'

Her lips parted. 'It's what you want, isn't it?'

Demetri's lips twisted. 'Oh, you have no idea what I want, Ms Lang.'

She sucked in a breath. Then, as if waking from a dream, she whirled away, shoving her bag into the filing cabinet and turning quickly back to the desk.

CHAPTER FOURTEEN

BUT almost against her will it seemed, her eyes were drawn back to his. 'What do you want, Mr Souvakis?' she asked a faint tremor evident in her voice. 'If you're looking for a one-night stand, I should tell you: I don't sleep around.'

Demetri couldn't help but admire her candour even if an involuntary exclamation spilled from his lips at her words. 'Nor do I, *thespinis*,' he said with mild indignation. 'And have I asked you to sleep with me? Forgive me, I do not recall making any such request.'

Her face flamed with hot colour now and he regretted being so blunt. Besides, if he was honest he'd admit that he had played with the idea of seducing her. More than played with the idea, dammit. He'd actually been anticipating it. That was really why he resented her perception.

'So—so long as we understand one another, Mr Souvakis,' she murmured primly, returning her gaze to her task, and Demetri knew an almost uncontrollable urge to prove to her how wrong she was.

But he made no response and after a few moments she apparently located the missing receipt. 'I knew I had it!' she exclaimed triumphantly, and Demetri, who wasn't at all interested in documentation that his assistant could collect just as easily, gave a mocking smile.

'I'll try and contain my excitement,' he remarked drily, and when she looked at him he saw her flush had deepened.

'It may not be important to you, Mr Souvakis,' she declared stiffly. 'But it's my job to see that each transaction is satisfactorily concluded. I'm sure your father wouldn't be happy without the necessary certificate of provenance for the sculpture.'

Demetri shrugged. 'I'm sure you're correct, Ms Lang. My father cares about such things, as you say.' He paused. 'Regrettably, I do not.'

'Then why did you offer to come and collect it?' she asked helplessly, and Demetri could no longer resist the urge to touch her.

'Because I wanted to see you again,' he admitted, acknowledging something that up till then he would have denied, vigorously. He ran his knuckles over the downy heat of her cheek. '*Apalos*. So soft.'

'But you said—' She jerked her face aside but she didn't move away. 'You said you didn't want to sleep with me.'

Demetri arched a lazy brow. 'Men and women do many other things besides sleep together, *thespinis*. Haven't you ever had a boyfriend?'

Her lips pursed. 'Of course I've had boyfriends.' She gave him a scornful look. 'I hope you're not going to pretend you want to be my boyfriend!'

'No.' He conceded the point. Then he grimaced. 'I do not consider myself a *boy* any longer.'

'So what are you saying?'

'Must I spell it out for you? I'd like to get to know you better. And then, if we find we are compatible, perhaps we will sleep together. Who knows?'

'I knew it!' She put some space between them and then

turned to face him with scornful eyes. 'That's all you're really interested in, isn't it? Why don't you admit it?'

'Because it's not true,' he retorted, his own anger sparking, and was amazed to find he meant it. 'Hell, do I seem like such a womaniser to you?'

'I don't know. I don't know you, Mr Souvakis.'

'Precisely. So before you start throwing insults around, perhaps you should give yourself a chance to find out.'

'I don't want to find out!' she exclaimed childishly, and Demetri felt his control slipping dangerously low.

'Are you sure about that?' he demanded, and, giving in to his baser instincts, he caught her wrist and hauled her against him. His arm wrapped around her waist and he looked down into her startled face with an unfathomable gaze. 'Are you really sure?'

For a moment she couldn't look away, but then, with a struggle, she managed to get a hand between them. Her fingers pressed insistently against his chest. 'Let go of me!'

'And if I don't?' Her slim bare legs duelling with his were a constant distraction. 'What will you do? You're alone here. You've virtually admitted as much.'

Her eyes darkened. 'Are you threatening me, Mr Souvakis?'

'No!' He was disgusted with himself for creating this situation. '*Poli kala.*' He released her. 'I suggest you give me the sculpture and I'll leave. As that seems to be what you want.'

'Yes.'

She agreed, though he thought there was a faint lack of conviction in her tone. Or perhaps that was just wishful thinking. She'd certainly not given him any reason to believe she was having second thoughts.

The parcel containing the sculpture proved to be bigger than he'd expected. 'It's all the packing,' she said ruefully, seeing his surprise. 'Can you manage?'

Demetri's lips twisted. 'Why? Are you offering to help me?'

Jane hesitated. 'If you wanted me to. I'm used to handling awkward packages.'

'And awkward customers, too,' he commented drily, and she linked her hands together at her waist and gazed at him with troubled eyes.

'I've offended you, haven't I?'

'*Hristo!*' Demetri swore. 'Why should it matter to you if I'm offended? You'll probably never see me again.'

'But I wouldn't like your father to think I'd been rude to his son.'

'Oh, right.' Demetri gave a short laugh. 'That's what all this is about, is it? You're afraid my father will take his custom elsewhere.'

Her shoulders lifted. 'I'm just an employee here, Mr Souvakis.'

'Well, don't worry.' Demetri grunted. 'My father would probably applaud your success in putting me in my place. He thinks I'm far too—what would you say?—arrogant as it is.'

Her lips twitched. 'You are.'

Demetri grimaced. 'Your humility didn't last long.'

She smiled. 'Perhaps that's because I like you better this way.'

'Making a fool of myself, you mean?'

She caught her breath. 'You couldn't make a fool of yourself if you tried.'

'No?'

'No.'

'Not even if I told you I wanted to kiss you right this minute?'

She stepped back from him. 'You wouldn't.'

Demetri shook his head and bent to pick up the box containing the sculpture. 'No, I guess this is where we go our separate ways.' He straightened, pulling a face at the weight of the package. 'D'you want to open the door for me? My car's just outside.'

'Oh—sure.' She hurried ahead of him through the darkened gallery and pulled open the glass door. 'You'll probably find a parking ticket on your windscreen. The attendants are pretty sharp around here.'

'I'll survive,' he remarked drily, turning sideways to negotiate the door and going down the steps to where a huge four-wheel-drive vehicle was parked at the kerb. 'Yeah, you're right.'

'Oh…' Jane followed him down the steps, going round the car to pull the pink slip from under the wipers. She looked at it impatiently. 'I'll ask Olga to handle this.'

Demetri had the boot open now and was pushing the heavy box inside, but he turned to say, 'Forget it. I will.'

'But you can't—'

'Want to bet?'

Jane bit her lip. 'This might not have happened if you hadn't helped me to carry those bags out and then—and then me cutting my finger…' She shook her head as he slammed the boot closed and came round the car to where she was standing. 'It's really my fault.'

'*Eh, then pirazi.* It doesn't matter.' He snatched the slip of paper out of her hand, screwed it up and tossed it into the nearest refuse bin. '*Oristeh.* I've dealt with it.'

She looked amazed. 'Is that what you do with all your parking tickets?'

'No. Only those I get by helping beautiful women,' he said mockingly, making her laugh. 'Don't worry about it.'

'You're—so—so—'

'Bad?' he suggested, checking the boot was locked and coming back to her. 'Yes, I know.'

'I wasn't going to say that,' she protested. 'I don't think you're bad!'

'But you don't like me.'

A look of confusion crossed her face and he realised she wasn't half as confident as she'd like to appear. And it would be so easy to take advantage of her here. The tree-lined avenue where the gallery was situated was quiet and shady, the sun rapidly sinking behind the buildings across the street.

But that wasn't going to happen. He wasn't about to destroy the fragile understanding that seemed to be developing between them and he was totally stunned when she suddenly put her hands on his shoulders and reached up to brush her mouth against his. 'I didn't say I didn't like you,' she said huskily, and Demetri could only slump back against the side of the car, too astonished to do anything else.

The kiss was brief, almost impersonal, but he knew she'd shocked herself, too. A look of consternation crossed her face and, although she hadn't yet turned to seek refuge in the gallery, he knew it was only a matter of time before she did so. Her eyes sought his in mute denial of what had just happened and Demetri arched an enquiring brow.

'I guess I did something right at last,' he remarked lazily, and she took a shuddering breath.

'I don't know what came over me,' she murmured and Demetri knew a kinder man might allow her to get away with that.

But he'd spent the last hour in a state of semi-arousal and her innocent appeal was the last straw. What did she think he was made of? Ice? Leaning towards her, he put his hands on her hips and pulled her against him. 'I do,' he told her, his voice thickening. 'Let me show you.'

He didn't give her time to protest. He kissed her as he'd been wanting to kiss her ever since he'd entered the gallery and seen her again. With one hand behind her head, he took possession of her lips, rubbing his mouth back and forward until the sweet scent of her breath showed her mouth was open and vulnerable.

To begin with, she tried to retain some control by bracing herself with a hand on the car at either side of him. But when he deepened the kiss, pushing his tongue deep into her mouth, she couldn't hold out any longer. With a little moan of acquiescence, she gave in. She sank against him, and he was sure she must be able to feel his erection pressing against her belly.

It was heaven and it was hell: heaven, because he wanted her so badly; hell, because, however eager she might be, he couldn't take her here in the street. Yet the urge to push her skirt up to her hips and bury himself in her soft heat was compelling, and, when she put a hand between them to stroke his throbbing arousal, he uttered an anguished groan.

'*Theos,*' he choked, aware that, despite the fairly explicit images he'd entertained himself with earlier, nothing had prepared him for this reality. It was just as well she was leaning against him, he thought. Her fingers were driving him insane.

But that was just part of it. The feel of her, the taste of her, the sensual delight in feeling her nipples peaking against his chest. She was so fiery, so responsive. All he could think about was getting naked with her, flesh against flesh, skin against skin.

That wasn't going to happen. No matter how adventurous she was out here, there was always the knowledge of the occasional passer-by to rescue her should it be necessary. Inviting her to accompany him back to an hotel room, however, was another matter entirely.

Yet once again it was Jane who amazed him. 'Let's go back inside,' she invited breathlessly. 'It's time I closed the gallery and Olga's got a half-decent sofa in her office…'

That had been the start of their affair, recalled Demetri grimly. And, despite her impulsive behaviour, he'd soon discovered that Jane had only slept with one other man. She was still hopelessly naïve, but hopelessly eager, deliciously inexperienced. She'd never had a true orgasm before, she'd confessed. Until then she'd believed that having sex was vastly overrated.

He'd soon corrected that error, he remembered a little smugly. The first time they'd made love—the first time he'd thrust into her hot, tight sheath—he'd had to silence her cries with his mouth. It had been one hell of an experience for both of them and he hadn't been able to wait before seeing her again.

Of course, there'd been obstacles. Both her mother and his hadn't approved. His own mother had been appalled when he'd told her he was falling in love with an English girl, and Jane's mother had never trusted him from the start.

But they'd overcome all objections, and, although he'd known Jane had been bewildered at the speed with which he'd made her his wife, she'd been too much in love with him to care. They'd honeymooned in the Caribbean, he reminisced painfully; long days and even longer nights on their own island, where all they'd done was eat, swim and make love. There hadn't been a lot of sleeping, he recalled, the memory as sharp and raw as ever. Dear God, how he'd loved her. He caught a breath. How he loved her still.

'Are you all right, Demetri?'

It was his father who spoke and Demetri realised he'd been staring out into the darkness beyond his windows for heaven knew how long. He'd been so lost in thought he'd forgotten that his father was waiting for him to make some response.

'I'm sorry,' he said, turning from the windows and pouring himself another drink. He needed the fortification, he thought, if he was going to get through this. 'I was just thinking, that's all.'

'About Jane?'

Demetri gazed at the older man with exasperated eyes. 'Can't I think about anything else?'

'I don't know. Can you?'

Demetri scowled. 'Leave it, Pa. If we go on with this, we're going to have words, and I don't want that.'

'Why? Because you think I can't be told the truth?' His father stared at him. 'Be honest, Demetri, why did you agree to divorce Jane and marry Ariadne? Was it only because you thought I was so desperate for a grandchild?'

Demetri sighed. 'Pa—'

'Answer me, dammit!'

'All right.' Demetri blew out a weary breath. 'All right. Maybe that was—a factor.'

'Your mother told you that, I suppose. Just as she told me that you and Ariadne had fallen in love, and Stefan that I would never recognise any child he and Phillippe might have as my own flesh and blood.'

'Stefan and Phillippe?'

'Yes.' Leo shook his head and held out his empty glass. 'Get me another drink, Demetri. You and I have things to say to one another, whether your mother likes it or not.'

CHAPTER FIFTEEN

JANE was alone in the gallery when Alex Hunter walked through the door.

For a moment she thought it was Demetri, and her heart leapt. She'd heard nothing from him since her return from Greece six weeks ago, and, although she'd told herself that was to be expected, she couldn't help wishing it wasn't so. She'd even tried to ring the villa on Kalithi, to assure herself he hadn't been hurt, but she'd never been able to get past Angelena.

She was sure Demetri's mother must have ordered the housekeeper to block her calls and, after a couple of knock-backs, Jane had given up. Besides, there'd been no further coverage in the Press, so she could only assume that both Demetri and his brother had returned from the fire unscathed.

She hadn't seen Alex since her return either, and that had been her decision. But, although she'd told him she didn't want to see him again, he wouldn't take no for an answer.

Lately, he'd accused her of making a fool of him, for letting him think they had a future together, when all she'd really wanted was to make her husband jealous. Which was patently untrue. But Jane had decided that, if that was what he wanted to believe, it might be for the best anyway.

If she'd expected he'd stop calling her, she'd been disap-

pointed, however. Her hopes that their relationship might go
back to the way it had been when he'd first come to the gallery
to audit Olga's books seemed doomed to failure. Now he was
here. He had no appointment with Olga today, so he couldn't
make that his excuse. In fact, her employer had left over an hour
ago, complaining of a headache and saying she was going
home to go to bed.

She wished she'd taken Olga's advice and closed the gallery
early. 'You work too hard for a woman in your condition,' Olga
had said, regarding the distinct swell of Jane's stomach with a
reproving eye. Ever since she'd learned her assistant was
pregnant, she'd been wonderfully supportive. Even if, like
Jane's mother, she didn't approve of her keeping the news of
the baby from the father.

Jane had intended to close the gallery, as Olga had suggested. But then the crates that had arrived that morning had
caught her eye. The carrier had opened the crates and left them
to be catalogued, and Jane had decided to spend another hour
with the canvases before closing up.

Now she wished she hadn't. She wasn't afraid of Alex, but
she would have preferred to meet him in a more public place.
If only Olga were still here, she thought, glad she was carrying
a clipboard. It enabled her to use it as a shield to hide her condition from him.

The knowledge that she was letting him intimidate her in
this way angered her. Which was why, when she spoke, there
was a slight edge to her voice. 'Hello, Alex,' she said, men-
tally squaring her shoulders. 'If you've come to see Olga,
she's—' she crossed her fingers '—she's gone out for a few
minutes.'

Alex gave a careless shrug of his shoulders. He was a fairly
tall man, but lean, his angular build not doing justice to his navy

linen jacket. 'It doesn't matter,' he said. 'It wasn't Olga that I wanted to see.'

Jane suppressed a groan. 'Oh, Alex—'

'I know. You've told me that you don't want to see me again—'

'I didn't say that, exactly,' murmured Jane, thinking of the gallery. 'I just don't think we should go out together any more. I thought we were friends, but obviously you wanted something else.'

'You did, too, before you went to see your ex-husband,' said Alex at once and Jane sighed.

'He's not my ex-husband yet,' she corrected him, not really knowing why she bothered. Just because she'd heard no more from Demetri's solicitors didn't mean the divorce wasn't going ahead. 'And that's not true, Alex. My relationship with Demetri hasn't changed.'

Alex regarded her disbelievingly. 'So why can't we continue seeing one another? I thought you liked me. I thought we had some good times together.'

'We did.' Jane could so do without this. She wrapped her arms about herself over the clipboard. 'It's just—well, I don't think it's fair to you to go on pretending that we'll ever be more than friends.'

Alex scowled. 'It apparently didn't matter to you before.'

'That was before you told me how you felt,' Jane reminded him unhappily. The clipboard was digging into her stomach and she adjusted it before continuing, 'I never intended to hurt you, Alex. Honestly.'

'But you have.' Alex shifted restlessly, and then, totally without warning, he snatched the clipboard out of her grasp. 'For goodness' sake,' he exclaimed, 'can't you put that damn thing down while we're talking?'

He flung the offending item onto the floor and it skittered away across the polished boards. He watched it go and so did Jane, though for different reasons. Alex looked as if he was trying to control his temper, whereas Jane just felt totally exposed now.

She was wearing linen trousers and a rose-patterned smock top that fastened beneath her breasts and flared over her waist-band. It was the kind of outfit lots of young women wore. It didn't necessarily spell pregnancy. But the swell of her stomach did. She'd always been so slender before and the distinct bulge was unmistakable.

It apparently was to Alex. His eyes seemed riveted to it. Jane was embarrassed. This was the last thing she needed. She wished he would just go and leave her alone.

'Are you pregnant?' he asked at last, in a dazed voice. Then, with some bitterness, 'I bet Demetri knows about this!'

'He doesn't.' Anger came to Jane's rescue. Walking swiftly across the floor, she bent and picked up the clipboard. 'In any case, it's nothing to do with you, Alex. I think you'd better go.'

Alex's brow furrowed. 'You haven't told Demetri he's going to be a father?'

'Did I say this baby was Demetri's?'

'No. But I just assumed—'

'You assume a lot of things,' said Jane tersely. 'Why don't you do as I asked you and leave?'

He didn't move. 'What are you going to do?'

'Excuse me?' Jane couldn't believe his audacity. 'I think that's my business, don't you?'

'Well, are you going to marry the baby's father? Whatever you say, it is Demetri's, isn't it?'

Jane gasped. 'You have no right to say that.'

'I assume that means you're not. Getting married again, I mean.'

'I am married and, as I said before, you assume too many things. Now, please, I want to close the gallery. I'd like you to go.'

Alex moved a little nearer. 'Don't be like that, Jane. I only want to help you.' He paused. 'I care about you. I still do, even if you have betrayed me with someone else.'

'I did not betray you.' Jane wished desperately that someone would come and interrupt them. 'Alex, this is silly. I'm sorry if you think I've misled you. But talking about it isn't going to change anything.'

'It could.' He was just a few feet away now. 'You could marry me instead. I think I'd make a good father. And a child needs a father, don't you agree?'

Jane was horrified. 'But I don't love you, Alex.'

'I know that.'

'Then—'

'I love you.'

'No—'

'I always have. Right from the first time I came here to do Mrs Ivanovitch's accounts. She knew how I felt. She was the one who told me what a pig your husband had been to you. She said I should just be patient. That sooner or later you'd realise I was nothing like him.'

Oh, Olga!

Jane closed her eyes for a moment, wishing her employer were there. Obviously the conversation Alex was talking about had taken place some time ago. If only Olga had been here, she could have explained that to him.

'I'm sorry,' she said again. 'I—I appreciate the compliment, Alex, I really do, but I can't marry you.'

'Why not?'

'You know why not.'

'No.' He shook his head. 'I don't think you've given the

matter enough thought. I know you don't love me now, but give it time. We'll have years to—'

'No, Alex.'

She spoke firmly, but all he did was move even closer and put his bony hands on her shoulders. 'Come on, Jane. Give me a chance. Let me show you how good it could be…'

'No, Alex.'

She was getting scared now. It was obvious she wasn't getting through to him and, whatever she said, he simply refused to listen to her.

'I don't think you appreciate the position you're in,' he went on, smoothing her arms in a way that made her skin crawl. 'A divorcee. A single mother. There aren't that many men who are prepared to take on another man's child.' He bent his head and, although she fought him, he succeeded in nuzzling her shoulder. 'Let me care for you, Jane. You know you want to.'

'I don't. Alex, please!' She pressed her hands against his chest, the clipboard falling between them. 'You have to let me go!'

'I don't *have* to do anything,' he retorted, moving in closer and pinning her back against an oil painting of the last tsar of Russia. It was one of Olga's favourites, and wasn't for sale, and the heavy gilt-edged frame dug painfully into Jane's spine. 'I can do what I like. Who's going to stop me?'

'Alex, for God's sake…'

Jane was losing hope. With the frame digging into her back and the clipboard digging into her ankle, she had never felt more helpless. And then she had an idea. She lifted her foot and kicked the clipboard hard into Alex's leg.

He swore, but for a moment his hold slackened and Jane took the opportunity it gave her. Shoving him away from her, she ran half sobbing towards the door.

The distinctive sound of the door opening halted her

headlong flight. It was late afternoon and the sun filtering through the blinds threw the visitor's face into shadow. All Jane could tell for certain was that it was a woman and her initial thought was that Olga had come back.

'Thank God you're here,' she got out unsteadily hurrying, towards her. 'Please—you must get Alex to leave me alone.'

'Alex?'

The voice was unfamiliar at first and Jane closed her eyes for a moment, praying she hadn't made a complete fool of herself in front of one of Olga's more influential clients. Then she opened her eyes again, realising she knew that accent. Ianthe Adonides of all people was standing staring at her, slim and elegant in a cream Chanel suit and pearls.

The house owned by the Souvakis family was in Bloomsbury. An elegant Georgian townhouse, overlooking Russell Square, it had three floors, a basement and an attic. It had once belonged to some minor member of the aristocracy, Jane remembered Demetri telling her. It had amused him to keep the area 'below stairs' for his own use.

Of course, that had been in the days when his mother and father had been frequent visitors to London. He'd first furnished the basement rooms when he was a teenager and that was where he'd taken Jane when they'd first become lovers. It was where he'd asked her to marry him, she remembered, her heart quickening instinctively. They'd been so happy in those days. How could she have let her own jealousy destroy what they'd had?

Why hadn't she believed him?

She asked the taxi driver to drop her at the corner of Bedford Place and walked the last few yards to the house she remembered so well. There were steps up to the glossy green door and a fanlight glowing with the light from inside. So someone was at home, she comforted herself. Of course, it could be just the housekeeper. Or even Theo Vasilis. Ianthe had told her she'd flown to England with both men, her growing relationship with Demetri's assistant the reason why she'd been invited along on what was primarily a business trip.

It was getting dark and, not wanting to be taken for a would-be intruder, Jane climbed the steps and rang the bell. Then, to give herself something to do while she waited, she checked that the belt of the loose-fitting woollen jacket she was wearing was securely tied about her waist. Until she was absolutely sure that Demetri wanted to see her again, her pride wouldn't let her use her condition to influence the outcome of this visit.

She seemed to wait for ages and only a grim determination forced her to stay the distance. Imagining Demetri checking some security monitor, and discovering it was her, tormented her. What if he refused to speak to her? What if what Ianthe had told her—that he and Ariadne were no longer seeing one another—simply wasn't true? Would she lie?

She'd certainly lied before.

The sound of a key turning put all these anxieties on hold. The deadlock was released and the door swung open on oiled hinges to reveal a rather plump, attractive woman in her late thirties. Jane's first devastating thought was that this was why Demetri and Ariadne had split up. He'd found someone else. But then the woman spoke and Jane realised that once again she was jumping to conclusions. Besides, Demetri would never allow a girlfriend of his to answer the door.

'May I help you?'

The woman's voice was polite, deferential, and Jane drew a breath. 'Um—is Mr Souvakis at home?'

The woman frowned now. 'Is he expecting you, Ms—Ms—'

'Souvakis,' said Jane at once and saw the way the woman's eyes widened with a mixture of surprise and disbelief. 'I'm— Mrs Souvakis. Demetri's wife.'

The woman blinked. Then, glancing nervously behind her, she murmured, 'I'm sorry. Mr Souvakis didn't tell me you were joining him.'

Jane wished she had the nerve to just walk into the house. But it was five years since she and Demetri had lived together and this woman didn't know her from Adam. Or should she say *Eve?*

'He's not expecting me,' she admitted uncomfortably. Then, in an effort to establish her identity, she added, 'Where is Mrs Grey?'

'Mrs Grey?' The woman looked a little less doubtful now. 'You know Mrs Grey?'

'Mr Souvakis' housekeeper, yes.' Jane nodded. 'Is she still here?'

'Mrs Grey retired three years ago,' the woman answered. 'I'm Mrs Sawyer. I took her place.'

'I see.'

Jane was feeling slightly reassured when a man's voice interrupted them. 'Who is it, Freda?' he called; from upstairs, Jane surmised. '*Ineh,* Theo? Tell him to come in.'

'It's not Mr Vasilis, Mr Souvakis,' Mrs Sawyer replied, raising her voice so he could hear, and Jane's heart almost stopped beating when she heard someone coming down the stairs.

'Well, you know I'm going out,' Demetri was saying as he reached the bottom of the stairs and strode along the hall towards the door. And then he saw Jane, and the silence that ensued was almost deafening.

'Hello, Demetri.' Jane knew it was up to her to say something. 'May I come in?'

Demetri exchanged a look with Mrs Sawyer. 'This is my

wife, Freda,' he said, unaware that they had already introduced themselves. Then, without meeting Jane's eyes, he stepped back and gestured her inside. '*Neh,* come in. I am going out, but I can spare you a few minutes. If it's urgent.'

'It is,' said Jane, giving the housekeeper an apologetic smile. The door closed and she nervously moistened her lips. 'How are you, Demetri? You look well.'

In actual fact, he looked anything but, she thought. The strain of his father's illness was obviously taking its toll on him. Ianthe had told her that Leo Souvakis was still alive, but very frail. Jane imagined he was very disappointed that Demetri's relationship with Ariadne had come to nothing.

Demetri didn't answer her and she wasn't really surprised. He must know she hadn't come here to enquire about his health. He was probably wondering why she was here, for, despite what Ianthe had said, he had made no attempt to see her during his visit.

'We'll be in the upstairs sitting room,' he told the house-keeper now. And then, after a moment's hesitation, 'Would you like coffee? Or something stronger?'

'Um—tea would be nice,' murmured Jane, still unable to face the former. 'If it's not too much trouble—'

'Tea. For one, Freda.' Demetri gave the order. Then, indicating the staircase, '*Parakalo:* you know where the sitting room is.'

Jane glanced behind her as she climbed the stairs. 'You—er—you don't live in the basement these days?' she asked, trying to lighten the mood.

'Freda and her husband have their apartment in the basement,' Demetri replied flatly. 'I haven't used it for years.'

'Oh.'

Jane couldn't think of an answer to that and instead tried to distract herself by familiarising herself with her surroundings.

Silk-lined walls, hung with priceless paintings, cushion-soft carpets, a crystal chandelier. And that was before she entered the family sitting room, with its Bokhara rugs and curved leather sofas, its elegant marble fireplace and exquisite works of art.

She paused in the doorway, where pocket doors could be slid aside to create a larger space for entertaining. When Demetri's father had been in London, the Souvakises had enjoyed a busy social life. Jane remembered parties where finding a guest without a famous name had been quite a feat.

She turned to remind Demetri of this, but he was already easing past her, crossing the room with the evident intention of getting himself a drink. And not tea, she speculated, aware that he looked much leaner than she remembered. Although his black pleated trousers and white silk shirt fitted him with glove-like precision, he had definitely lost some weight. There was more grey in the sleek beauty of his hair now and surprisingly he needed a haircut.

'So,' he said, at last, turning to rest his hips against the cabinet behind him. He was holding a glass with what she suspected was whisky in it. 'To what do I owe this unexpected appearance?'

Jane came slowly into the room. 'I notice you don't say "unexpected pleasure",' she said lightly, resisting the urge to wrap her arms about her waist. Then, because it was easier than getting to the real point of her visit, 'How is your father?'

'He's—as well as can be expected, isn't that what they say? Thank you for asking.' He paused. 'But you could have rung the villa and found that out for yourself.'

Jane didn't think so, but she didn't want to get into that now. Instead, she let a little of her emotions show. 'Oh, Demetri—'

'Please.' The look he directed towards her would have chilled an ice cube. 'You can't turn up out of the blue and expect a welcoming committee. Not after leaving Kalithi as soon as my back was turned.'

Jane's jaw dropped. 'It wasn't like that.'

'No? You knew Stefan and I were flying out to the *Artemis*. Didn't it occur to you that it might be dangerous?' He gave a short laugh. 'Or didn't you care?'

'Of course I cared.'

'*Psemata?*'

'Yes, really!' she exclaimed. 'But you knew I couldn't stay there indefinitely.' She was reluctant to mention his mother's part in her departure, but there was something she could say. 'I did ring the villa after I got back to England, but—well, I couldn't get through.'

Demetri's lips twisted. 'Do you expect me to believe that?'

'It's the truth!'

'So why couldn't you get through? Had you forgotten the number?'

'Of course not.' Jane sighed. 'Perhaps Angelena didn't understand what I wanted.'

Demetri's scepticism was evident and, in another attempt to explain her behaviour, she said unhappily, 'Ariadne resented me, you know she did.'

Demetri's brows drew together. 'Did Ariadne say something to make you leave?'

'N…o.'

'I thought not.'

'Demetri, please—'

'Please what?' He swallowed the remaining liquid in his glass in one gulp and turned to refill it. Then, with his back to her, he said, 'What do you want, Jane? Are you worried because I've let the divorce stall these last few weeks?' His shoulders rounded. 'You have to understand, I've had other things on my mind.'

'I know that.' Jane drew her lower lip between her teeth.

Then, because she had to know if Ianthe had been telling the truth, 'Are you still seeing Ariadne?'

He swung round then, his expression violent. 'What's it to you?' he demanded harshly. 'You don't care what happens to me.'

'I do!' Jane couldn't let him think that, even if his response was no answer. 'I've never stopped caring about you.'

Demetri was bitter. 'Then you have a bloody funny way of showing it.' He shook his head. 'Why don't you tell me what this is all about and get it over with?' He glanced at the slim gold watch circling his narrow wrist. 'I've got a dinner engagement in exactly forty minutes.'

'Ianthe came to see me.'

Jane hadn't intended to be so direct, but it was too late now. He was staring at her with hard, disbelieving eyes and she wondered painfully if the Greek girl's confession had come too late, also.

'*Apokliete!*' he muttered at last. No way!

'It's true.' Jane gazed at him despairingly. 'She—she came to the gallery. She told me that you and Ariadne were no longer together.'

'Ariadne and I have not been *together,* as you put it, since I came to your apartment over three months ago,' he told her coldly. 'That should hardly be news to you.'

Jane was confused. 'I don't know what you mean.' She frowned. 'When I arrived in Kalithi, Ariadne let me think—'

'That she and I were sleeping together?' Demetri was bitter. 'And you, of course, believed her.' He spread his arm dramatically. 'My wife,' he said contemptuously, 'who still thinks I'll sleep with any woman who'll have me.' He downed another mouthful of his whisky. 'And you say you care about me. Forgive me if I say that's bloody pathetic!'

CHAPTER SIXTEEN

THE arrival of Mrs Sawyer with Jane's tea gave Demetri a few minutes to compose himself. He was tempted to pour himself another drink, but the knowledge that getting drunk—again—wouldn't do him any favours made him set down his empty glass with a heavy thunk.

Jane, meanwhile, had accepted the housekeeper's suggestion and seated herself near the table where Freda had put the tray. But he noticed she made no attempt to drink the tea the woman had poured for her and Freda, after assuring herself that they had everything they needed, took it upon herself to close the doors as she left the room.

Realising he had to make some attempt to rescue the situation, Demetri forced himself to take the chair opposite his wife. Then, balled fists digging into his spread thighs, he said tersely, 'I suppose Ianthe told you she'd flown to England with Theo Vasilis and myself?'

Jane nodded. 'Yes.'

And that would be another strike against him, Demetri reflected malevolently. Had she really come here to challenge him again about something that had never happened?

He scowled. It didn't help that she was looking particularly lovely this evening. There was a glow about her, somehow, an inner warmth that made him curse the mess he'd made of both their lives. He'd never stopped wanting her, never stopped loving her. Even when he'd told himself he hated her, he'd known it was just his own pitiable need that was driving him on.

Her hair was longer, he noticed, his eyes devouring every item of her appearance. One strand curled invitingly over the shoulder of her woollen jacket; he wished she'd take the jacket off. He was a fool, he knew, but he wanted to see her breasts. They'd always been such a giveaway of the way she was really feeling.

Jane was aware that Demetri's eyes had slipped down her body and she felt the heat of his dark gaze like a fire against her skin. He'd always had this effect on her and never more so than tonight. Knowing what she did about him, knowing he had never lied to her, knowing what a stupid fool she'd been.

'You say Ianthe came to the gallery,' he prompted at last and she nodded again.

'That's right.' Then, rather than get to the point of her visit, she launched into an explanation of what had happened. 'It was just as well she did,' she said fervently. 'Alex was there—Alex Hunter, that is—and he was being a nuisance.'

Demetri's eyes narrowed. 'A nuisance? How?'

She should have been warned by the comparative mildness of his tone, but Jane was so relieved that he was talking civilly to her that she went on. 'Oh—in the usual way,' she said ruefully. 'He—well, he wouldn't accept the fact that I didn't want to see him again. Socially, I mean. If—if Ianthe hadn't come into the gallery as she did—'

'You are saying this man—this *cur*—molested you?' Demetri swore, springing to his feet with a violent oath of frustration. 'I will find him and I will kill him! How dare he lay a hand on my wife? I will make him wish he had never been born!'

Jane couldn't sit still with him towering over her. 'Am I still your wife, Demetri?' she whispered, rising to face him, and he looked at her with dark, avenging eyes.

'For the present,' he muttered harshly, subduing the urge he had to touch her. 'In any case, that is not important. This man, Hunter, will learn that no one assaults a member of my family and gets away with it.'

'He didn't—assault me, Demetri.' She sighed. 'He frightened me, that's all.'

'*Aliti!*' Bastard! Demetri swore again, raking restless fingers through his hair. 'So this time I must be grateful to Ianthe for her intervention, no?'

'Yes.'

'Ironic, is it not?'

'Perhaps.' Jane swallowed and gestured towards the sofa. 'Could we sit down again? I've got something to tell you.'

'And you think perhaps it will rob me of the strength to stand on my own two feet?'

'No…'

'Because I warn you, Jane, if you've come here to spread more of Ianthe's poison—'

'I haven't!' She put a nervous hand on his arm, feeling the muscles clench beneath her fingers. 'Please, Demetri, you have to listen to me.'

Demetri looked down at the hand resting on his arm and wondered how that tentative touch could spread an electric charge throughout his body. The desire to touch her in return, to touch her and taste her and feel that slim, lissom body yielding to the pressure of his caused an actual constriction in his chest. His pulse was racing, his heartbeat quickening in concert with his rising blood pressure. *Theos,* how the hell was he going to compose himself sufficiently to attend a business dinner in the Souvakis boardroom in less than half an hour, when all he could think about was taking her to bed?

'All right,' he said at last through clenched teeth, and she withdrew her hand and subsided onto the sofa again.

He lowered himself into the seat beside her, resisting the urge to crowd her. Even so, when she moved, her thigh was disturbingly close to his, and once again he was tempted to remind her of all they had once been to one another.

For her part, Jane was intensely aware of him watching her. His gaze fairly burned her skin and she permitted herself to run a reassuring hand over her stomach before going on.

She'd had her first scan a few days ago and seeing the baby's image on the monitor had brought a tight lump to her throat. Her mother had been with her and she'd been a great support, but Jane had wished Demetri could have been there. It was his baby, just as much as it was hers, and didn't he deserve to know he was going to be a father? But at that time, she'd believed he and Ariadne were planning their own future and how could she ruin his life for a second time?

'Well?'

Demetri was getting impatient and Jane leaned forward and took a nervous gulp of the cooling cup of tea. Then, composing herself, she said, 'I expect you're wondering what I could possibly have to say that would interest you?'

Demetri's mouth turned down. 'You think?' he queried sardonically. 'I thought you might be going to commiserate with me for not being able to sustain a lasting relationship, but I suppose that would be—how do you say?—pushing it, no?'

Jane sighed. 'Don't be sarcastic!'

Demetri's expression darkened. 'Then tell me how I'm supposed to be,' he snapped. 'Or is this just another game of provocation?'

'It's not a game.' Jane played with the belt of her jacket. 'I—still haven't told you why Ianthe came to see me.'

Demetri stiffened. 'I thought she wanted to tell you that Ariadne and I were no longer sleeping together.'

Jane's lips tightened. 'Must you be so crude?'

'*Theos,* you sound just like my mother.' He scowled. 'But she did give you reason to doubt what Ariadne had told you?'

Jane shook her head. 'Yes—'

'That's something, I suppose.'

'But in all fairness, you told me you'd slept with Ariadne,' said Jane defensively.

Demetri groaned. 'I'm not a monk, Jane.'

'I know that.'

'Oh, right. You know this because I made Ianthe my mistress just months after we got married?'

He would have got up from the sofa then but, with more courage than she'd given herself credit for, she reached out and gripped his wrist. His arm was lightly covered with dark hair but she could feel the heat emanating from him, the racing pulse beneath the skin.

'Don't go,' she said, her voice husky. 'Ianthe's told me what happened. About her baby, I mean. That—that Yanis was the father, not you.'

For a moment he just stared at her and she had no idea what he was thinking. There was such a wealth of bitterness in his gaze that she felt herself shrink from the accusations she felt sure he was going to make.

'Ianthe told you?' he said hoarsely. '*Theos,* why would she do that?'

Jane moistened her dry lips. 'I'm not entirely sure,' she admitted huskily. 'Perhaps it had something to do with the fact that you and Ariadne had split up.'

'What did my relationship with Ariadne have to do with Ianthe?'

He was bewildered and showed it and Jane desperately wanted to comfort him. But she had the feeling he wouldn't welcome her sympathy right now. 'I think,' she said, choosing her words with care, 'that she'd realised you weren't going to be happy with—with anyone else—'

'But you, you mean?' he demanded savagely, and this time she had no chance of stopping him when he wrenched his wrist out of her grasp and got to his feet. 'My God!' He strode across to the long windows that overlooked the square below. 'And I'm supposed to be grateful for this?' He turned to look at her, contempt in his eyes. 'Damn you, Jane, I don't want your pity!'

'I don't pity you, Demetri.' Herself, maybe. She got to her feet and started towards him, but his gaze speared her like a knife and she halted uncertainly. 'Please, you've got to listen to me. I know I've been a fool—'

'You got that right.'

'—but what was I supposed to do?'

Demetri's lips twisted. 'You could have believed me.'

'Yes, yes, I could.' Jane shook her head. 'That sounds so simple, doesn't it? I should have believed you, when the only other person involved insisted you were to blame.'

'Ianthe lied.'

'I know that now.' Jane held up her head. 'But you have to admit, no one—not even your father—told me who the baby's father really was.'

Demetri hunched his shoulders, running his hands up to grip the back of his neck. 'It was difficult for them, too,' he muttered.

Jane felt indignant now. 'I'll bet.'

'Yanis was just starting his training to become a priest.'

Demetri spoke heavily. 'There was no way he could have continued with his studies in those circumstances.'

'He should have thought of that before he slept with Ianthe!'

'I agree.' Demetri cast her a look out of the corners of his eyes. 'Believe me, he was left in no doubt that his behaviour had shamed him, shamed the family.'

'Not to mention your part in it,' said Jane forcefully. 'And, by extension, mine.'

'It wasn't meant to be that way.' Demetri was vehement. 'No one expected Ianthe to tell everyone that I was to blame.'

Jane's brows drew together. 'But I thought…' She tried to regroup. 'No one but you ever denied it.'

Demetri nodded. 'That was my mother's doing, I'm afraid.'

'What do you mean?'

'Oh…' His hands fell to his sides. 'It all happened a long time ago now.'

'That's no answer.'

'*Endaxi.*' All right. He turned to face her, spreading his arms in a gesture of defeat. 'You know my mother was always opposed to our marriage. When Ianthe said what she did, my mother persuaded my father and Stefan that denying it would only turn the spotlight on Yanis. Ianthe had spent a lot of time at the villa that summer. You know that.'

'Don't I just?' Jane found it hard to hide her resentment.

'*Oristeh.*' There you are. Demetri's tone was flat. 'It seemed it was the only way to save Yanis's future.' He sighed. 'And I, poor fool that I was, thought you'd believe me when I told you it wasn't my child. That our marriage was strong enough to withstand anyone's lies.'

'You could have told me the truth,' Jane insisted. 'Not just that you weren't to blame, but that Yanis was really the baby's father.'

'*Neh,* you're right. I could have done that.' Demetri regarded her sombrely. 'But, you know what? I had some pride in those days. And I was so sick that you could even think that of me after everything we'd been to one another that I thought, what the hell! Let her believe what she likes for now. In time, she'll see she was wrong.'

Jane stared at him. 'You expected me to stay, knowing how I felt?'

'*Veveso!*' Sure. 'That's what people do when they love one another. They try to work things out. It never even crossed my mind that you might leave me!' He groaned. '*Theos,* I thought we loved one another.'

'We did. I did. I did love you.' Jane was near to tears. 'And I'm not saying I didn't regret it afterwards. But you have to understand what it was like for me, too. I asked Ianthe—I begged her to tell me the truth—and she said you'd only married me on the rebound. That you and she had always cared about one another, and that that was why your mother had always opposed our marriage—'

'But that's—rubbish!' Demetri swore then. 'I was never interested in Ianthe and she knows it. She was in love with Yanis. She used to follow him around like a pet sheep. When she found out he was going to be a priest, I think she was desperate. She'd have done anything to stop him. Including throwing herself at him, I assume. And let's face it, Yanis was young, and flattered, *pithanon.* I dare say he had no idea what she had in mind.'

Jane's knees felt weak. 'If only you'd told me.'

'If only you'd told me you were leaving,' he countered savagely. 'Do you have any idea what it was like for me, coming home from a business trip to find my wife had gone to London and, according to my mother, she wasn't coming back?'

Jane pressed her lips together. 'I might have known your mother would play a part in it.'

'Yeah, well, I was devastated. If it hadn't been for my work, I think I'd have gone out of my mind.'

Jane swallowed. 'You could have come to see me. You could have told me about Yanis.'

'Oh, Jane!' Demetri sank down onto the wide window seat and leaned forward, his forearms braced on his thighs. 'Do you really think I didn't try?'

Jane was confused. 'I don't understand…'

'When it became obvious that you weren't coming back, I did try to see you, Jane. Several times. But both your mother and the Ivanovitch woman insisted you didn't want to see me.'

'No—'

'*Neh.*' He was adamant. 'I left messages on your mother's answering machine asking you to meet me. I even hung about outside the gallery, hoping I might be able to intercept you when you left. But you either slipped out the back or you avoided me in some other way.'

'I didn't know.' Jane was pale. She tried to think. 'I did stay with my mother when I first got back, and I did go to work at the gallery, as you say. I don't know how we could possibly not have seen one another.'

And then, she did. 'Oh, God,' she breathed. 'I think I know what happened.'

She remembered how, at that time, she'd been less than enthusiastic when Olga had suggested a trip to New York. She'd only been back in England for a few days and all she'd really wanted to do was hide away and lick her wounds. Getting on a plane to New York, being expected to talk business with the gallery Olga dealt with, had seemed totally beyond her.

But Olga had been so disappointed at her reaction that she'd eventually given in. She'd decided it was just Olga's way of trying to help her, of giving her something to do that would take her out of herself and give her time to deal with her pain in an environment that held no unhappy memories.

Now she recognised Olga's actions for what they'd really been. An attempt on her part, and probably on Jane's mother's, as well, to get her out of London and away from Demetri.

Demetri had been watching the play of emotions that had crossed her face as the truth dawned. But when she quickly explained what had happened, his reaction was not what she'd expected.

'So,' he spoke with resignation, 'Ianthe and my mother weren't the only ones who wanted to keep us apart.'

'No.' She gazed at him. 'I'm sorry.'

'*Neh,* so am I.' He slumped then, burying his face in his hands. '*Theos,* this is too much for me to handle.' His nails raked over his scalp. 'All this time I thought you were happy with the situation.'

Jane caught her breath. 'I thought you were.'

He looked up then. 'How could you think that?'

'How could I not?'

Demetri stared at her for a long time, then he gave a weary sigh. 'So, now we know the truth at last. That's something, I suppose.'

Jane felt sick. 'Is that all you have to say?'

'What do you expect me to say, Jane?' he demanded, bitterly. 'Do you think I am happy that I had to find out like this? All these years, all the lies people told—' He made a helpless gesture. 'I don't even know what you want from me now. Understanding? Absolution? Exoneration? You've got them. But I have to tell you honestly, I'll never forgive myself.'

'Oh, Demetri…' Jane couldn't stand the suspense a moment longer. Covering the space between them, she gazed down at his bent head with burning eyes. Then, she laid her hand on the

back of his neck and discovered his hair was damp with the
sweat that was pouring out of him. It was all the encourage-
ment she needed to say softly, 'Will you ever forgive me for
doubting you? For allowing other people to make such a mess
of our lives?'

Demetri didn't immediately answer her, but he groped for
her blindly, pulling her between his legs and burying his face
against her stomach. Then, in a strangled voice, he said, 'I'm
the one who needs your forgiveness, *aghapi*. If I hadn't been
such a—pigheaded fool, you wouldn't have run away.'

Jane's hands came up to cradle his head against her. 'I wish
I hadn't,' she whispered unsteadily. 'I wish I'd stayed. I wish
I'd made Ianthe tell me the truth.' She broke off, her voice
thick with emotion. 'I never stopped loving you, you know.
Even when I thought I hated you, I knew it was because you
could still hurt me so much.'

Demetri tipped his head back and gazed up at her. 'Do you
mean that?' he asked hoarsely, but he could tell from the tears
in her eyes that she did. '*Theos!*' He pressed his face against
her again to hide his own ragged feelings. 'I can't believe it.'

'I wouldn't lie to you,' she said, taking his face between her
palms and tilting it up to hers. She bent and bestowed a lingering kiss on his parted lips. 'Does that convince you?'

Demetri's eyes searched her face. 'So you'll stay with me?
You'll come back to Kalithi with me and be my wife?'

'If that's what you want.' Jane was trembling, as much from
the knowledge that his head was pressed against their baby as
from her relief at knowing that he cared about her still. 'If you
love me, that is. If you believe we have a future together.'

'If I love you!'

Demetri came to his feet in an instant, grasping her shoulders and pulling her roughly into his arms. He gazed down at

her, his eyes dark and intimate. Then he kissed her and even the air was suddenly hot and thick with emotion.

'If I love you,' he muttered again, taking the lobe of her ear between his teeth and biting it painfully. 'Of course I love you. Why do you think I didn't let Gerrard handle the divorce for me? He wanted to. He said it wasn't a good idea for me to spend time with you again. And why do you think I wanted to see you, to have you come out to Kalithi, if it wasn't that I couldn't get you out of my head?'

'But your father—'

'Oh, yes. My father was eager to see you again. I'm not denying that. But he knew what I was doing. That was why he was so angry with me at times. Because he knew I still cared for you and I wasn't being honest with either Ariadne or myself.'

Jane touched his cheek. 'I was so jealous of Ariadne,' she admitted.

'You didn't have to be. Once I'd seen you again, I realised what a poor substitute Ariadne was.' He paused. 'But I have to admit, when I came back to the island a couple of days after the explosion on the *Artemis* and found you'd gone again, I was shattered. I couldn't believe you'd walked out on me again.'

'But your father must have told you what happened.'

Demetri shook his head. 'Or course, you don't know. My father was ill when I got back to Kalithi—' And when Jane made an anxious interjection, he raised a reassuring hand to cup her cheek. 'I think it was the shock of the explosion, minor though it was, that kept him in his bed for a few days. By the time he was up and about again, I'd gone back to Athens.'

'To Athens?'

'Yes.' Demetri pulled a wry face. 'I didn't have to, but I had to get away from the island. Once again, I think it was only my work that kept me sane. I couldn't eat; I barely slept; I was consumed with guilt and misery. Stefan was worried about me. I think he thought I was going to drink myself into an early grave.'

Jane stroked his cheek. 'I've been such a fool.'

'You don't have the monopoly on that, believe me,' Demetri assured her fiercely. His hands slid beneath the collar of her jacket, caressing the soft skin at her nape. 'I should have told you the truth about Ianthe as soon as I realised I still cared about you. But you seemed so—distant; so—in control; so—happy with your life.'

'Oh, Demetri.' Jane shivered as his hands moved over her shoulders and then tugged at the tie that kept her belt in place. 'You only had to touch me and I was on fire. Don't pretend you didn't realise it, that day you came to the apartment.'

He smiled. 'Whether you believe it or not, I didn't come to your apartment expecting to tumble you into bed.' He brushed his lips over hers and she quivered. 'I was sure you wouldn't want to see me and I was fully prepared for you to hear what I had to say and then throw me out.'

'Me, throw you out?' Jane was incredulous.

'Well, not physically, maybe, but you know what I mean. I really thought you'd be glad to be free of me at last.'

Jane's eyes widened. 'Did you really think that?'

Demetri grimaced. 'If you want the truth, I don't think I thought any of it through until I saw you. Then I realised why my mother had been so against me having any part in the divorce. She must have known how I'd feel when I saw you again.'

'And how I'd feel, too,' murmured Jane huskily. 'Oh, God, when you came into the bathroom, I just wanted to die!'

'And I just wanted to hold you,' said Demetri, tipping the woollen jacket off her shoulders and letting it fall to the floor. 'As I want to hold you now,' he continued, gazing down at her.

'Come—let me show you how much I want you. How much I'll want you for the rest of our lives.'

'But—your dinner engagement—'

'Theo can handle my dinner engagement.' His eyes darkened. 'Do you honestly think I'm going to leave you now?'

Jane hardly remembered the main bedroom suite at the townhouse. She and Demetri had only used it a couple of times in the past when Mrs Lang had been away. Jane's mother would have been offended if they hadn't accepted her hospitality, even if she'd lost no opportunity in those days to criticise Demetri's privileged way of life.

Now Jane looked about her, noticing the décor had all changed, cream and gold giving way to much more masculine tones. 'Ariadne never stayed here,' Demetri said softly, coming into the room behind her and sliding his arms about her midriff. 'I know what you're thinking, but our relationship never extended beyond the island.'

'I expect she stayed at your house there,' said Jane tensely, expecting him to notice her thickening waistline any moment.

'No.' Demetri was distracted, his lips finding the racing pulse below her earlobe. 'On those occasions when I sought Ariadne's bed, it was always at the villa.'

'I—I don't know if I want to know that.' Jane's voice was unsteady. 'I don't want to think of you making love to someone else.'

'Having sex with someone else,' Demetri corrected her gently. 'The only woman I've ever made love with is you.'

'I—well, there's been no one else in my life,' she confessed and Demetri blew softly into her ear.

'You have no idea how much pleasure that gives me, *aghapi mou,*' he told her thickly. 'I am a selfish man, I know, but I would have found it very hard to be complacent about something like that.'

Jane tilted her head back against his shoulder. 'Chauvinist!'

'I am. I admit it.' He turned her to face him. 'Can you forgive me?'

'I'll think about it.' She gazed up at him with adoring eyes. 'Oh, Demetri, do you realise that if Ianthe hadn't got a conscience at last, we might never have seen one another again?'

Demetri lifted his hands to her breasts. 'I don't believe that.'

'Why not? You're here in London and you've made no attempt to see me, have you?'

'I've seen Gerrard,' he admitted huskily. 'I've told him I don't want to continue with the divorce.'

Jane's eyes widened. 'You have?'

'Yes.' He looked rueful. 'I know what I said earlier, but I'd already decided that, if you wanted the divorce, you would have to come and see me.'

Jane knew an overwhelming sense of satisfaction, but then another thought occurred to her. 'What about your father?'

'My father knows how I feel about you,' he said simply, his fingers going to the ribbons that secured her smock. 'We had a long conversation, he and I, and he told me that my mother had led him to believe that Ariadne and I were in love.' He sighed. 'She'd also told Stefan other stuff about my father but that needn't concern us now.'

'About the fact that your father would never recognise any child of Stefan's as his grandchild?'

Demetri's brows descended. 'How do you know that?'

'Stefan told me.' She lifted her shoulders appealingly. 'We got quite close while you were away in Athens. He told me he was very hurt that his father seemed to have so little faith in him.'

'Really?' Demetri absorbed what she'd said. Then, 'Well, things are going to change. And they'll change even more when he learns I'm making him my deputy.'

Jane's eyes widened. 'Is that your father's idea?'

'No, it's mine.' Demetri was smug. 'I have no intention of risking our relationship as I did before. In the past weeks, I've realised that work is good if you've got nothing else in your life. But I do now. I have you. And your happiness is going to be my number-one priority from now on.'

'And does Stefan agree?'

'He will, when I tell him. He'll understand how ticked-off I feel knowing that while you were on the island my brother spent more time with my wife than I did.'

Jane's lips parted. 'You're jealous!'

'Yes. Yes, I am. Bloody jealous, as it goes,' he agreed thickly. He bent to brush her cheek with his tongue, kissing the soft flesh on the underside of her jaw before trailing his mouth to the scented hollow between her breasts. He loosened the ribbons. 'I want you all to myself.'

The sides of the smock fell apart and Demetri's lips sought the swollen peaks of her breasts pressing against the cream lace of her half-bra. '*Oreos*,' he whispered. Beautiful. '*Saghapo*.' I love you. He took one nipple into his mouth, suckling her through the cloth, causing a wave of longing that spread from her breasts to her stomach and from there to the place between her legs that was already wet and throbbing with need. '*Se thelo*,' he added huskily. 'I want you.'

'Oh, God, Demetri,' she choked, clinging to him urgently, and he tore one hand away to take off his tie and rip open the buttons of his shirt.

His chest, with its dark triangle of hair, brushed against

skin that was already sensitised to an unbearable pitch, and Jane decided that telling him about the baby could wait just a little longer…

Their lovemaking was wild and uncontrolled. Demetri had intended to take it slowly and deliberately, to enjoy every moment of it, but as soon as he felt her tighten around him, her muscles squeezing him and demanding his release, all his good intentions flew away. He wanted her. He needed her. And they would have plenty of time in the months and years to come to perfect something that was already as near perfect as it could get.

Tearing the coverlet aside, he pulled her to the bed, peeling off his own clothes as he did so. Jane seemed to share his urgency, for she shimmied out of her trousers and it was his pleasure to remove the rest of her clothes as he caressed her.

Then he was inside her and she was so ready for him. Feeling the slickness as he filled her with his thick shaft almost achieved his objective, but he wanted her with him every step of the way.

Jane drew up her knees and pressed the soles of her feet into the mattress, giving her the leverage she needed to push up against him. But when he would have drawn away to taste her, she dug her nails into his shoulders and urged him on. She wanted him, all of him, and the ripples of her own orgasm demanded his total possession.

And it was good, so good. Better than ever because this time there was no possibility that anyone would interrupt them. They had all evening and all night to explore the delights of their reunion, and, when Jane's climax swept her away, she heard Demetri's groan of satisfaction echoing her own.

It was dark when Jane opened her eyes again. It took a moment to adjust to the shadowy light that filtered in from the street-lights outside. But she had barely done so before a lamp was

illuminated and she realised Demetri had been lying, propped
on his elbow, watching her as she slept.

'Hi,' he murmured, regarding her with undisguised satisfaction. He bent to brush his lips across the soft curve of her
jawline. 'I thought you were going to sleep forever.'

The dark stubble on his chin grazed hers and she blinked up
at him in some surprise. 'What time is it?'

'About half-past-twelve,' he told her softly. 'Why? Are
you hungry?'

'Hungry?' Jane's hand sought her stomach and then, remembering, she licked her dry lips. 'I—no. Not particularly.'

'Sure?' Demetri turned and when he came back he was
holding a glass of wine in his hand. 'How about thirsty? I'm sorry
I don't have any champagne, but the Chardonnay is fairly good.'

'Um…' Jane shuffled up against the pillows, realised she
was completely naked and reached automatically for the sheet.
'Not for me, thanks.'

Demetri frowned, instantly aware of her uncertainty. '*Ti
simveni?*' He shook his head and spoke in her language.
'What's wrong?'

'Nothing's wrong, exactly.'

Demetri was really worried now. Putting the wine aside, he
turned to sit cross-legged beside her, and, although Jane knew
this wasn't the time to be provocative with him, she couldn't
prevent herself from putting her hand between his legs.

He hardened instantly, and her tongue circled her lips in
helpless anticipation. Oh, God, she thought, she loved him so
much. How could she have wasted so many years because of
her foolish pride?

'What is it?' he demanded, but she noticed his hand held
hers against him. 'Tell me, Jane, before I go completely out
of my head.'

Jane hesitated. 'You know what you said about—about wanting me all to yourself?'

'Yes.' He was wary now.

'Well, how would you feel if I told you that six months from now that was going to change?'

Demetri frowned. 'I don't—' He broke off shaking his head. 'What are you saying? That you want—who—your mother, maybe, to come live with us?'

Jane had to smile then. 'No, not my mother, silly!' she exclaimed fiercely. She looked down at herself and then, with some hesitation, drew the sheet away. 'Haven't you noticed anything different about me? Don't you think I've put on a little weight since—since the last time we made love?'

Demetri stared into her eyes for a moment, then his gaze dropped to her stomach before lifting to her face again. *'Theos,'* he said in a shaken voice. 'You're pregnant!'

'Mmm.' Jane was nervous. 'How do you feel about it?'

'How do I feel?' Demetri rolled onto his knees and leant towards her, his hands cradling her stomach. 'How do I feel?' he echoed unsteadily. 'I'm…' His voice shook. 'I'm—staggered!' He tried to gather his thoughts. 'When were you going to tell me about this?'

Jane trembled. 'How could I tell you? I thought you were going to marry Ariadne.'

'Hristo, Jane, you knew why I was marrying Ariadne!'

Jane shook her head. 'I know. But—so much had happened. I couldn't bear the thought that you might think I had only got pregnant to ruin your life for a second time.'

'Not telling me about this baby would have ruined my life,' Demetri assured her forcefully. *'Theos,* a baby! I'm going to be a father! I can't believe it.'

'But—you're—happy about it?'

Demetri cupped her face in his hands and pressed a hungry kiss to her open mouth. 'I'm not just happy,' he told her thickly. 'I'm freakin' ecstatic! My wife! My baby! *Theos,* it doesn't get any better than this…'

EPILOGUE

NIKOLAS DEMETRI LEONIDES SOUVAKIS was born on Valentine's Day. He weighed in at a massive ten pounds five ounces, and Jane was pale but triumphant when her in-laws came to view the new arrival.

Demetri had been with her throughout the twenty-four hours of her labour. And, although at times he would have opted for a Caesarean, Jane had wanted to have their son naturally, wanted Demetri's hands to be the first the baby felt on his arrival into the world.

It was wonderful that Leo could be there to hold his grandson, too. Actually, in recent months, since he'd welcomed Jane back to Kalithi again and learned of her pregnancy, he seemed to have acquired a second lease of life. And despite her opposition to their reunion, even Demetri's mother had been unable to hide her pride that she was going to be a grandmother at last.

Stefan, too, had been to see his nephew, but now he'd flown to England to bring Jane's mother and sister back for a visit. Even Mrs Lang had been persuaded that her daughter had never been happier, and, because there was going to be a new baby visiting her house, she was much more tolerant of her other grandchildren's antics than she had used to be.

Olga, meanwhile, had sent a message expressing her delight

at the news. She would come out to see the baby on one of her frequent buying trips to Greece. Jane knew Olga was hoping that one day she'd reopen the gallery in Kalithi, but that would be a long time in the future, if at all.

Jane's mother and Lucy had arrived and welcomed the new baby, but now they'd returned to the villa and the suite of rooms Angelena had prepared for them. It had been agreed that all guests should stay at the villa and not with Jane and Demetri. Her daughter-in-law needed rest, Maria Souvakis had insisted, for the first time considering Jane's feelings before her own.

It was much later that night before Jane and Demetri were alone together. Jane had slept for a while and then taken a shower, and when her husband came into their bedroom she was looking deliciously relaxed and rested in an ivory satin nightgown with tiny pearl buttons down the front. Demetri thought she'd bloomed in the last six months, and their happiness was palpable.

'Tired?' Demetri asked now, coming to sit on the side of the bed nearest his wife, and Jane stroked his cheek.

'A little,' she conceded. 'But I'll get over it. How about you? You haven't even been to bed.'

Demetri shrugged. 'I don't like sleeping alone,' he confessed softly, playing with the buttons on the front of her gown.

'You don't have to,' she said at once, moving across the huge bed to give him room. 'Come on. You know you want to.'

Demetri hesitated. 'You need your sleep,' he said, glancing at the clock.

'You need yours,' she countered. 'I want you to stay, Demetri. I don't like sleeping alone either.'

Demetri regarded her for a long moment and then he stood and unfastened his shirt. Tossing it onto a chair, he followed it with his trousers, and then drew back the covers to get into bed.

'You don't sleep in boxers,' Jane pointed out huskily, and, with a rueful grimace, Demetri kicked them off as well.

'Goodness knows what Nurse Seledha will say when she brings Nikolas for his feed,' Jane added, teasingly. And when Demetri would have protested, she reached over him and turned off the lamp. 'Don't fret, my darling. She'll just be envious of me.'

Mediterranean Men

Let them sweep you off your feet!

Gorgeous Greeks

The Greek Bridegroom by Helen Bianchin
The Greek Tycoon's Mistress by Julia James
Available 20th July 2007

Seductive Spaniards

At the Spaniard's Pleasure by Jacqueline Baird
The Spaniard's Woman by Diana Hamilton
Available 17th August 2007

Irresistible Italians

The Italian's Wife by Lynne Graham
The Italian's Passionate Proposal by Sarah Morgan
Available 21st September 2007

*...International affairs, seduction
and passion guaranteed*

VOLUME FOUR

The Tycoon's Princess Bride
by Natasha Oakley

Isabella Fierezza has always wanted to make a
difference to the lives of the people of Niroli and she's
thrown herself into her career. She's about to close
a deal that will ensure the future prosperity of the
island. But there's just one problem…

Domenic Vincini: born on the neighbouring, *rival*
island of Mont Avellana, and he's the man who can
make or break the deal. But Domenic is a man with
his own demons, who takes an instant dislike to
the perfect Fierezza princess…

*Worse, Isabella can't be in the same room with him –
without wanting him! But if she gives in to temptation,
she forfeits her chance of being queen…and will tie
Niroli to its sworn enemy!*

Available 5th October 2007

THE ROYAL HOUSE OF NIROLI

...International affairs, seduction and passion guaranteed

Volume 5 – November 2007
Expecting His Royal Baby by Susan Stephens

Volume 6 – December 2007
The Prince's Forbidden Virgin by Robyn Donald

Volume 7 – January 2008
Bride by Royal Appointment by Raye Morgan

Volume 8 – February 2008
A Royal Bride at the Sheikh's Command by Penny Jordan

8 volumes in all to collect!

FREE!

4 Books
and a surprise gift!

We would like to take this opportunity to thank you for reading this Mills & Boon® book by offering you the chance to take FOUR more specially selected titles from the Modern™ series absolutely FREE! We're also making this offer to introduce you to the benefits of the Mills & Boon® Reader Service™—

- ★ FREE home delivery
- ★ FREE gifts and competitions
- ★ FREE monthly Newsletter
- ★ Exclusive Reader Service offers
- ★ Books available before they're in the shops

Accepting these FREE books and gift places you under no obligation to buy, you may cancel at any time, even after receiving your free shipment. Simply complete your details below and return the entire page to the address below. You don't even need a stamp!

YES! Please send me 4 free Modern books and a surprise gift. I understand that unless you hear from me, I will receive 6 superb new titles every month for just £2.89 each, postage and packing free. I am under no obligation to purchase any books and may cancel my subscription at any time. The free books and gift will be mine to keep in any case.

P7ZEF

Ms/Mrs/Miss/Mr ....Initials.............................
BLOCK CAPITALS PLEASE
Surname ....
Address...

....Postcode ....

Send this whole page to:
UK: FREEPOST CN81, Croydon, CR9 3WZ